William Archer

Masks or Faces?

a study in the psychology of acting

William Archer

Masks or Faces?
a study in the psychology of acting

ISBN/EAN: 9783337396763

Printed in Europe, USA, Canada, Australia, Japan

Cover: Foto ©Andreas Hilbeck / pixelio.de

More available books at **www.hansebooks.com**

MASKS OR FACES?

A STUDY

IN THE

PSYCHOLOGY OF ACTING

BY

WILLIAM ARCHER

LONDON

LONGMANS, GREEN, AND CO.

AND NEW YORK : 15 EAST 16th STREET

1888

CONTENTS.

MASKS OR FACES?

CHAPTER I.

INTRODUCTORY.

To the average intellect, nothing is so alluring as a paradox. The reason is simple : in accepting a paradox, the average intellect feels that it has risen above the average. Any fool can believe what is possible and probable, but it demands no ordinary gifts, whether mental or spiritual, to believe what is absurd. How 'many an old philosophy' has been based, like an inverted pyramid, on an almost imperceptible point of paradox! How many a world-embracing creed has sprung from a tiny contradiction in terms ! What is a miracle, indeed, but a paradox in action.? He who has seen a table dancing a hornpipe, or an elderly gentleman reclining on the ceiling instead of on the sofa, naturally feels a certain superiority over the humdrum folk who have seen no miracles save those of Mr. Maskelyne. And if it seems a distinguished thing to believe a paradox, what must it be to invent one? Surely the summit of human ambition.

B

The paradoxes of philosophy generally prove, on analysis, to be contradictions in terms ; those of art, on the other hand, are more often truisms turned inside out. This I believe to be a fair description of Diderot's celebrated *Paradoxe sur le Comédien.* It undoubtedly contains a great deal of truth ; but in so far as it is true it is not paradoxical. The paradox is brought in, sometimes in the shape of sheer over-statement, more often by means of a little nimble jugglery with ambiguous terms and misleading ana-logies. In his arguments from analogy, Diderot does not rise to the fine frenzy of some of his fellow-theorists. 'We no more think feeling a necessary ingredient in acting,' cries one, 'than we should deem it expedient for a painter, after he had finished a like-ness upon the canvas, to represent the heart, liver, brains, and the internal formation, on the back of it.' Another—this time an American—executes a still more surprising feat of logical legerdemain. 'Did Rosa Bonheur,' he asks, with withering emphasis, 'feel like a horse-fair when she painted her great picture on that subject ? Or did Longfellow feel like "foot-prints on the sands of time" when he wrote that line of the *Psalm of Life?*' Diderot would no doubt admit that the zeal of these disciples outruns their discretion ; yet they merely burlesque some of his own arguments.

Not even the firmest believer in Diderot—not even M. Coquelin, who says, ' Je tiens que ce paradoxe est la vérité même '—will deny that the philosopher founded his doctrine on slender evidence. A few

*Oxberry, i.
p. 223*

*The Voice,
x. No. 3*

*L'Art et le
Comédien,
p. 24*

anecdotes, of doubtful interpretation, are all that he
advances in support of it, and Grimm expressly tells
us that for years before he formulated his theory he
had gone but rarely to the theatre. ' Able as he was,'
a distinguished actress writes to me, ' Diderot, both in
his *Paradoxe* and elsewhere, spoke without that intimate knowledge which only actors of the highest
order can possess.' For a fruitful discussion of the
points at issue, the interlocutors should be, not, as in
Diderot's dialogue, a dogmatic ' First ' and a docile
' Second,' but a trained psychologist and an experienced and versatile actor. Mr. H. D. Traill, in his
New Lucian, has given imaginary effect to this idea
in a suggestive dialogue between George Henry Lewes
and David Garrick. Had these two men ever met in
the flesh, with a stenographer behind the screen, their
colloquy would certainly have been luminous, if not
conclusive. Yet the evidence of one actor, though it
were Garrick himself, is obviously insufficient. There
are exceptional temperaments as well as exceptional
talents, and no one man is entitled to make a dogma
of his own experiences and methods. We want to
arrive at the laws which govern the average or typical
mimetic temperament ; and to this end we must study
as large a circle as possible of individual cases.
Imagine David Hume in the green-room of Garrick's
Drury Lane, with a royal commission to cross-examine
His Majesty's Servants severally and collectively, and
you have a nearer approach to the ideal conditions of
inquiry.

The discussion is not of the first importance ; but

since it has been started, and has led (in my judgment) to much false logic and empty paradox-
mongering, I have long thought that, in the interests
of 'lucidity,' a careful investigation should be attempted.   I am but an amateur psychologist, and
the reasonings contained in the following pages may
often stand in need of revision ; but at least I have
brought together a far larger body of evidence than
has hitherto been presented.

My endeavour has been to collect, both from
biographical records and from the communications of
living artists, the views and experiences of 'actors of
the highest order.' I believe, however, that not only
'actors of the highest order,' but every intelligent
artist who studies himself and others, has a right to
be heard upon the questions at issue.   I have therefore drawn no invidious distinction between the
greater and the lesser lights of the theatrical firma-
ment, but have accepted for what it is worth every
ray of illumination that has reached me.   Diderot
might object that his theory applies only to the
greatest actors ; that he does not deny that second-
rate actors feel and depend on feeling ; nay, that he
expressly affirms it.   If we define the great actor as
'he who does not feel,' all controversy is of course at
an end, for Diderot is safe in the inexpugnable fortress
of a circular argument.   But if we define the great
actor as 'he who powerfully affects his audiences';
if we learn that many of the greatest actors (in this
sense) confess to feeling acutely, and are observed by
themselves and others to exhibit many symptoms of

acute feeling, some of which are quite involuntary, and are of no direct use in heightening the illusion ; if we discover that in all grades of the art the majority of players find by experience that they tend to produce a better effect when they play from the heart than when they play from the head alone ; if we can find, in certain laws of mental and physical action and reaction, a rational explanation of this tendency ; and if we can ascertain with tolerable clearness the artistic checks and limitations to which it must be subjected—then, surely, we shall have made a considerable breach even in the irregular and baffling bastions of Diderot's position. To this end we should hear not only Hamlet but the Player King, not only Romeo and Juliet but Friar Laurence and the Fiery Tybalt.

The Editor of *Longman's Magazine* most courteously did all in his power to further my inquiry, and considerable portions of the present work first appeared in the numbers of that Magazine for January, February, and March 1888, under the title of *The Anatomy of Acting*.

In setting about the investigation, my first effort was, of course, to get rid of ambiguities. To ask, ' Do you feel in acting ? ' or ' Do you identify yourself with the characters you represent ? ' or ' Do you find sensibility an advantage or a disadvantage ? ' would only be to obscure the issue. It would have required a whole treatise to define, with anything like precision, the meaning I proposed to attach to these phrases, and I could not reasonably expect my obliging informants to study a disquisition on psychology. Moreover, even if I had succeeded in defining my terms, it would have been folly to expect in the general run of actors such habits of minute and accurate introspection as would enable them to give a lucid and trustworthy account of their experience. How, then, could I hope to arrive at practical results? Clearly, by confining my queries to outward symptoms, while reserving to myself the task of interpretation. A tear, a blush, or a tremor is an external, visible, sensible fact; an instance of presence or absence of mind is a subject for ordinary testimony ; a device or process for gaining a particular artistic end can be observed and described like any other action or series of actions. It was to these external details that I directed my informants' attention. I neither expected nor desired, of course, that they should refrain from stating their own inferences and interpretations, but it was the facts themselves with which I was chiefly concerned. These once collected in sufficient numbers, I trusted that by comparing, classifying, and interpreting them I might throw some light on the mental processes involved in mimetic art.

The interrogatory which I originally issued will be found in the Appendix. Subsequent experience showed that it was not so aptly worded and arranged as it might have been ; nevertheless it served its purpose. My own criticisms on it are implied in the alterations I made when preparing the French version (also reprinted in the Appendix), for which I am indebted to my friend Miss Blanche J. Taylor, of Paris.

How comes it, the reader may ask, since the questions were translated into French, that the experiences of living French actors are so meagrely represented? In explaining this, I shall be able to answer incidentally one or two objections to my method of inquiry.

As I could scarcely expect the leading artists of France to be at the pains of answering an interrogatory issued by an unknown Englishman, I forwarded to M. Francisque Sarcey a proof of my pamphlet, expressing a hope that he would call attention to it in his feuilleton in *Le Temps.* M. Sarcey, to whom my name was not quite unknown, met this request with a polite but firm refusal. 'Je regarde le procédé,' he wrote, 'qui est américain, comme fâcheux à la critique et à l'art.' I made no attempt, of course, to alter M. Sarcey's determination, but I respectfully laid before him my own view of the 'procédé.' It was this : The inquiry has no bearing whatever on criticism, which is concerned with the effect produced, not with the phenomena accompanying its production. If an actor can convincingly represent emotion, the critic, as a critic, need not inquire whether he experiences or mechanically simulates it. But criticism is one thing, the psychology of art another ; and to this the question at issue belongs. It is more curious than important, granted ; but several eminent men, from Diderot to Mr. Irving, have held it worth discussion, so that an attempt to inquire into it systematically

can scarcely be altogether idle. Nor is it quite without practical importance. Sensibility can be culti-
vated or it can be crushed, like any other gift of
nature. It is quite conceivable that a young actor
may help or hinder the due development of his powers
by starting with a right or with a wrong theory as
to the artistic value of real emotion. Idiosyncracy,
indeed, will generally determine his theory, but sheer
intellectual conviction may not be without its effect.

It is true—and this may have been in M. Sarcey's
mind—that by concentrating attention on individual
symptoms of emotion the spectator may become
insensible to the whole emotional impression of a
performance. He 'cannot see the wood for trees.'
While in the thick of my inquiry, I was conscious
that this preoccupation displaced my point of view,
so to speak, and interfered with my normal recep-
tiveness. In my own case, the effect has already
quite worn off; and I can scarcely fear (or hope) that
the reader of the following pages will find his mental
attitude towards the stage seriously or permanently
affected by the considerations they suggest. If this
book were in the hands of every playgoer, if the
questions it discusses were vividly present to the
minds of any large percentage of an average audience,
then indeed my inquiry might be 'fâcheux à la
critique et à l'art.' Such a disaster, I own, would
have its consolations for me, if not for M. Sarcey.
The fear of it, at any rate, does not disturb my sleep
o' nights.

Repulsed by M. Sarcey, I applied to another

distinguished Parisian critic, but he too declined to assist me. I do not mention his name, because the reasons he gave were more frank than flattering to the artists whose work he criticises. He did not believe, he said, that my inquiry would lead to any trustworthy result, because few actors had the intelligence, and none the sincerity, to answer my questions aright. This objection has been urged in more than one quarter; indeed Diderot himself advances it. 'You may prove my theory to demonstration,' he says, 'and a great actor will decline to acknowledge it; it is his secret. A middling actor or a novice is sure to contradict you flatly.' The experience of actors gained in the course of my investigation leads me to dissent entirely from Diderot and my Parisian correspondent. My questions were answered, whether verbally or in writing, always, I believe, with perfect sincerity, and generally, I am sure, with perfect intelligence. When it happened that a question was misunderstood, the fault, as a rule, was mine rather than my informant's. Some, of course, answered with more insight, more precision, in short more ability, than others; but I seldom received a reply that was altogether beside the mark. Many artists to whom I sent my 'catechism' lacked time or inclination to respond; but of those who favoured me with their experience not one proved deficient either in intelligence or in earnestness. On the latter point, of course, my opinion must be taken for what it is worth, sincerity being, in the nature of things, incapable of proof. I had now and then to allow for the 'personal

Pollock p. 15

equation,' but of wilful insincerity I discovered no trace. Where, indeed, is the motive for it? Once upon a time there might have been a tacit conspiracy among actors to keep what Diderot calls 'their secret' and prevent the outside public from suspecting the hollowness of their emotional displays. If this trick of the trade was ever practised, it has obviously broken down. Great actors—a few, but a very respectable few—proclaim the 'secret' to the four winds of heaven; middling actors, so far from 'flatly contradicting' Diderot, are found to swear by him. Diderot himself has made insensibility honourable. It is an unmistakable distinction to belong to the intellectual few who act from the brain alone. If there is any motive for insincerity, it now operates in Diderot's favour; but, though constantly on my guard, I discovered no trace of wilful deception in either sense. My informants even resisted the temptations to levity which, I admit, were offered them.

The attitude of M. Sarcey and his colleague convinced me that there was little hope of obtaining answers from the leading artists of Paris. Accordingly I did not issue my French interrogatory. Only one or two stray copies of it found their way across the Channel.

As loose quotation too often introduces confusion and error into arguments of this nature, I have in almost all cases given exact references to my authorities. I have also done my best to trace anecdotes to their sources, and to avoid the more or less garbled

forms which they are apt, in course of time, to assume.
In this I have not always succeeded. Anecdote-
tracking is a difficult sport, and those who have most
experience of it will most readily excuse an occasional
failure to follow up the true scent. I do not pretend
to have ransacked thoroughly the theatrical literature
even of England and France for evidence upon the
points under discussion. A complete collection of
the documents in the case would fill ten volumes
rather than one. All I can hope to have accomplished
is a fairly representative selection of anecdotes and
opinions. Where no reference is given, the reader
will please understand me to draw upon manuscript
authorities in my own possession—either notes of
interviews or written answers to my printed questions.
In quoting from the *Paradoxe* I have always referred
to Mr. Walter Herries Pollock's useful translation,
but I have in some cases given my own rendering of
Diderot's text, for the sake either of brevity or of
literalness. I am further indebted to Mr. Pollock for
allowing me to make use of his copy of Sticotti's very
rare booklet, the peg on which the *Paradoxe* is hung.

After a careful search for less cumbrous expressions, I have been forced to fall back upon the terms
' emotionalist ' and ' anti-emotionalist ' to indicate the
contending parties in this dispute. They are pain-
fully clumsy; but the choice seemed to lie between
them and still clumsier circumlocutions.

*London :
Chatto &
Windus,
1883*

CHAPTER II.

HISTORICAL.

THE controversy is entirely modern. The ancients, so far as I can discover, had no Diderot. They have left us a few anecdotes and remarks (to be quoted hereafter) all tending to show that the emotional theory held the field unquestioned. Far more explicit and weighty are the utterances of Shakespeare, who, as it seems to me, went to the root of this matter and has said what might well have been the last words upon it. But in his time there was no controversy. The emotional theory, under due restrictions, was accepted as self-evident. It was in France, about the middle of last century, that the present dispute arose.

In 1747, Remond (or Rémond) de Sainte-Albine, one of the editors of the *Mercure de France*, published a treatise called *Le Comédien*. It discussed in a · rambling and unsystematic fashion the qualifications necessary for an actor, together with certain questions of technique. M. Remond was an emotionalist, thorough-going and unashamed. He writes as though the need for 'sensibility' had never been called in question. His effort is to determine the precise

¹, pp. 78, 167

admixture of 'understanding,' 'sensibility,' and 'fire' requisite for the perfect actor ; but the idea of altogether banishing sensibility never enters his head. The following extract from his table of contents is sufficient to show that he carried his emotionalism to the verge of absurdity :—

'LIVRE II. : *Section I.*

'Chapitre I.—La gaieté est absolument nécessaire aux Comédiens, dont l'emploi est de nous faire rire.

'Chap. II.—Quiconque n'a point l'âme élevée, représente mal un héros.

'Chap. III.—Si toutes les personnes de Théâtre ont besoin de *sentiment*, celles qui se proposent de nous faire répandre des larmes, ont plus besoin que les autres de la partie du sentiment, désignée communément sous le nom d'*entrailles*.

'Chap. IV.—Les personnes nées pour aimer devroient avoir seules le privilège de jouer les rôles d'Amans.

Such propositions as these appear to me, I confess, not only to touch, but to overshoot, the verge of absurdity ; yet I hesitate to dismiss contemptuously a book which Lessing mentions with respect.

Near the close of his *Paradoxe*, Diderot remarks :— 'For the rest, the question I am diving into was once before started between a middling man of letters, Remond de Sainte-Albine, and a great actor, Riccoboni. The man of letters pleaded the cause of sensibility ; the actor took up my case. The story is one which has only just come to my knowledge.'

Hamburgische Dramaturgie, June 23, 1767
Pollock, p. 83

It is evident that Diderot speaks from hearsay, not having himself seen the documents; and I think he confounds Luigi Riccoboni the father with François Riccoboni the son. The father, who alone could be called a great actor, was an uncompromising emotionalist. He published in London, in 1725, a poem entitled *Dell' Arte Rappresentativa : Capitoli Sei,* dedicated 'A Sua Eccellenza My Lord Chesterfield.' He was too intent on his triple rhymes to make his doctrine very clear or exhaustive; but on the question of sensibility the following passage is perfectly explicit :—

Capitolo Secondo

Per seguitare il naturale instinto
   E moversi senz' Arte or che s' ha a fare
   Scordare i quatro membri, e forse il quinto,
Che è la Testa ; ma si ben cercare
   Di sentire la cosa, che ci esponi,
   Che si creda esser tuo l' altrui affare.
D' Amor, di Sdegno, o Gelosia li sproni
   Se al Cor tu provi, o s' anco pur sarai
   Qual Oreste invasato da Demoni ;
E l'Amore, e lo Sdegno sentirai,
   E Gelosia, e Belzebu germani,
   Senz' Arte braccia, e gambe moverai.
Ed io scommetterei, e piedi, e mani,
   Che un sol non troverai, che ti censuri
   Fra tutti quanti li fidei Christiani
Se con il Cuore i tuoi moti misuri.

Paris, 1738

P. 20

P. 31

Again, in his *Pensées sur la Déclamation,* Riccoboni warns the orator not to work up tears, but to make no effort to repress them if they arise naturally. '*Sentir ce que l'on dit,*' he says emphatically, '*voilà les tons de l'âme.*' François Riccoboni, on the other hand, after due protestations of perfect filial respect, takes the liberty of flatly contradicting his father. In his book called *L'Art du Théâtre* he maintains the necessity of absolutely repressing the physical symptoms of emotion. He gives two reasons : the difficulty of governing the voice, and the impossibility of passing from one passion to another with the rapidity required under the artificial conditions of the stage. 'S'il tombe une seule larme de vos yeux,' he says, 'des sanglots involontaires vous embarrasseront le gosier, et il vous sera impossible de proférer un seul mot sans des hocquets ridicules. Si vous devez alors passer subitement à la plus grande colère, cela vous sera-t-il possible ? Non, sans doute.' In these arguments Diderot is clearly, though incompletely, anticipated. It appears that Riccoboni's work was written before Sainte-Albine's, though published later ; otherwise he might have gone into the question more fully. He seems to have published a second treatise on the same subject some years later, but I have not been able to procure it. As Diderot professes to have no personal knowledge of Riccoboni's productions, they do not enter into the genealogy of his ideas.

Paradox begets paradox ; and we could scarcely have a wilder paradox than the assertion that none but a magnanimous man can act magnanimity, and that lovers alone can do justice to a love-scene. Sainte-Albine's budget of paradoxes was the direct progenitor of Diderot's, though there are two intermediate stages in the pedigree. Three years after *Le Comédien* appeared in Paris, an anonymous Englishman published an adaptation of it under the title

Paris, 1750

P. 37

London,
1750

Lowe, p. 2

Feb. 8,
1749–50

of *The Actor: a Treatise on the Art of Playing.*
The book has generally been attributed to Aaron
Hill, the adaptor of Voltaire's *Zaïre, Alzire,* and
Mérope; but as the sequel, published in 1755, is
expressly stated to be 'written by the Author of
the former,' and contains allusions to events which
occurred after Aaron Hill's death, this attribution must
be incorrect. Whoever the author may have been, he
made as little as possible of his obligations to Sainte-
Albine, mentioning them in such ambiguous terms that
their true nature seems to have escaped notice from
that day to this. As a matter of fact, the whole theoretical portion of· *The Actor* is simply translated from
Le Comédien. For example, the chapter-headings
quoted above are literally reproduced, as well as the
arguments they summarise. The adaptation, however,
is, if not an abler, at least a more entertaining book than
the original. Sainte-Albine dealt far more in precept
than in example. Indeed he is curiously chary of
anecdote and illustration. The adaptor, on the other
hand, lost no opportunity of pointing his moral by
references to the plays and actors of his own day—
Quin, Garrick, Barry, Mossop, Macklin ; Mrs. Cibber,
Mrs. Pritchard, Peg Woffington, and Kitty Clive. We
are indebted to him for some of our clearest information as to the methods of the ' palmy days.' ·In 1755,
as I have said, a sequel or second edition was published, under the same title. It professed to be ' A
New Work. . . . Adapted to the Present State of the
Theatres,' but was in truth a mere recapitulation
of the former argument, with some new anecdotes

inserted. Though his use of Sainte-Albine's work showed a deficiency in psychological acumen as well as in literary ethics, the nameless writer (' an author unknown to you, and who shall ever remain so ') was certainly no fool. He was well read ; he wrote a very fair style ; and, theories apart, he was an excellent critic of acting.

Here the matter may be said to have rested for fourteen years, until, in 1769, Antonio Fabio Sticotti, who seems to have been an actor of the Italian com- pany in Paris,[1] bethought him to re-adapt into French the English adaptation of Sainte-Albine's work. Sticotti, however, seems to have had no suspicion that *The Actor* was not entirely original. The fact that he makes no mention of Sainte-Albine might possibly be due to an underhand design of giving his book a false air of novelty ; but in that case he would cer- tainly have taken some pains to lessen the similarity between the two treatises. As it is, *Garrick, ou les Acteurs Anglois* bears the most evident marks of its descent : a similar design, similar theories, similar arguments. For instance, the four chapter-headings quoted on p. 13 are replaced by the following, unnum- bered, but in the same order :—

'De la Gaieté nécessaire à l'Acteur Comique.'   *Ed.* 1770, *pp.* 123-146
'De la Noblesse d'ame nécessaire à l'Acteur Tragique.'
'De la Tendresse.
'Du Penchant à l'Amour.'
Sticotti, indeed, gave most of his attention to the

---

[1] On the Sticotti family, see *Campardon*, ii. p. 144.

C

anecdotic side of his English original, translating
many anecdotes, and (in foot-notes) adding parallel
cases from French stage history.   Thus Sainte-Albine
himself might not at the first glance have recognised in *Garrick* a grandson of his own *Comédien.*
Amid all changes, however, his emotional extravagances were faithfully reproduced ; and it is to
these that we owe the anti-emotional extravagances

Assézat,
xix. p. 387

of Diderot and his followers.   In a letter to Mdlle.
Jodin, dated some years before the appearance of
Garrick, we find Diderot expressing himself a convinced emotionalist.   ' Si, quand vous êtes sur le théâtre,' he writes, ' vous ne croyez pas être seule, tout est
perdu. . . . Un acteur qui n'a que du sens et du juge-
ment est froid ; celui qui n'a que de la verve et de la
sensibilité est fou.   C'est un certain tempérament de
bon sens et de chaleur qui fait l'homme sublime ; et
sur la scène et dans le monde, celui qui montre plus
qu'il ne sent, fait rire au lieu de toucher.'   After this,
we can scarcely be wrong in attributing the extreme
anti-emotionalism of his later position to the reaction
begotten by emotionalist excesses.

Sticotti's work became highly popular.   At least
three editions were published in three consecutive years,
and a German translation appeared in 1771.   The
German translator may have been put on the track of
the booklet by a somewhat elaborate criticism of its

Assézat,
viii. p. 339

theories contributed by Diderot, in 1770, to Monsieur
Grimm's *Correspondance.* ' Un homme illustre dans les

Ed. 1770,
p. xi

Lettres,*' says Sticotti in his preface, ' aimé autant

* .Monsieur Diderot.—[Sticotti's note].

qu'estimé pour sa politesse et l'humanité de ses sentimens, a bien voulu m'avouer que mon livre lui avoit fait *naître de bonnes idées.* Je conviens que s'il m'eût été permis de les employer, j'aurois été certain de réunir tous les suffrages de mes Lecteurs.' Little did he think that Diderot's 'good ideas,' which, with polite contempt perhaps, he insisted on keeping to himself, ran in flat contradiction to the whole tenor of his book. They made 'good copy,' however, for Grimm's princely clients, and the essay contributed to the *Correspondance* contains the entire gist of the subsequent *Paradoxe.*

It was probably in 1773 that Diderot remodelled his essay in the form of a dialogue, adding new anecdotes and instances, but in no way modifying his theoretical position. An allusion to a miraculous actress playing, at seventeen, the heaviest tragic parts, is taken to refer to Mdlle. Raucourt, who made her first appearance September 23, 1772. It has since been discovered that, like other Infant Phenomena, she had remained stationary at sweet seventeen for several years. There are allusions, also, to events which occurred in 1776 and in 1778 ; so that Diderot must evidently have retouched it, perhaps more than once. As was his habit with many of his writings (*Le Neveu de Rameau* is a notable instance) he took no steps to publish it. The draft of 1770 was first printed as part of Grimm's *Correspondance* between 1812 and 1814. The completed *Paradoxe* did not see the light till 1830.

CHAPTER III.

THE 'PARADOXE.'

THE dialogue, as a form of exposition, has this disadvantage, that it stimulates the pugnacious, or, more politely speaking, the chivalrous instinct in human nature. One of the disputants invariably goes as a lamb to the slaughter, and his pre-arranged massacre · cannot but stir our sympathy. Thus a feeling of antagonism to the writer's argument is aroused by the very form. There is a cat-and-mouse cruelty about the Socratic method against which our sense of justice, nay, of humanity, rebels.

In few expository dialogues—I need not, surely, insist on the distinction between an exposition in form of argument and a merely fanciful or satirical colloquy—in few expository dialogues do we feel the imperfection of the form more keenly than in Diderot's *Paradoxe*. One of its chief paradoxes is that the second speaker is practically dumb. He now and then bleats forth a semi-articulate objection ; but he evidently knows that he is there to be slaughtered, and is anxious to get the operation over as soon as possible. Acting upon Grimm's favourite maxim, ' Ne vous expliquez point si vous

voulez vous entendre,' he never thinks of demand-
ing that unpleasant preliminary to all fruitful debate : a definition of terms.   Why, then, does
Diderot, who must have known (none better) that
Grimm's maxim was a mere pleasantry, ensconce
himself behind it in order to enjoy an empty triumph
over an imaginary opponent?   For the very reason,
I suspect, that he was not satisfied with his own argument.   That he believed himself right in the main is
not for a moment doubtful ; but re-reading his hasty
sketch of 1770, he felt, I think, the lack of system in
his ideas, and chose at once to disguise and to excuse
it by recasting the little treatise in dialogue form.
He says himself, 'I have not yet arranged my ideas   *Pollock,*
logically.'   To have undertaken a systematic psycho-   *p.* 8
logy of acting would have led him too far afield.
He probably did not think the subject worth the
trouble.   Besides, he wanted to kill two birds with
one stone : to refute the heresies of Sticotti (or rather
of Sainte-Albine) and to hint at the absurdities of
French classic tragedy.   That the latter object was
present to his mind no one can doubt who reads the
Paradoxe carefully, in connection with Diderot's   *Morley, i.*
other writings on the drama.   He was a ' naturalist '   *p.* 328
(I do not mean a Zolaist) born out of due time.   He
foresaw the modern drama and he believed in it,
though his own attempts to realise it were not
encouraging.   When we find him, then, as in the
Paradoxe, assuming throughout that the personages
of the stage must necessarily be ' magnified and non-
natural men,' can we help suspecting him of laughing

Pollock,
p. 12

Pollock,
p. 19

in his sleeve ? Yet that is the groundwork of his whole contention, so far as it can be reduced to any sort of unity. Agamemnon and Orestes, Cleopatra and Agrippina, according to his own illustration, are like the ghosts which children manufacture with the aid of a sheet, a broomstick, and a gruff voice. These spectres neither move, speak, nor think like men ; why should they weep like men ? That is the gist of the argument, and so far it is logical enough ; though it is not quite clear that a certain thrill of real emotion might not help the actor to rise to the 'magnified and non-natural' emotion of his personage. But supposing this thesis absolutely right, what does it amount to ? Not a fundamental principle of art, but a commentary (not to say a satire) upon French tragedy. And no one, I think, knew this better than Diderot. How else are we to read such a passage as this ?—

' LE SECOND : C'est que peut-être Racine et Corneille, tout grands hommes qu'ils étaient, n'ont rien fait qui vaille.

LE PREMIER : Quel blasphème ! Qui est-ce qui oserait le proférer ? qui est-ce qui oserait y applaudir ? '

He was sincere in his admiration for Corneille and Racine, but Lessing himself had scarcely a lower opinion of the form in which they worked.

I know not how better to display the multitudinous meanings which Diderot attributes to 'sensibility' than by taking the place of ' The Second ' speaker and interjecting a few comments upon the main positions of 'The First.' My quotations shall be accurate so far as they go ; if the reader suspects me of doing Diderot injustice in wrenching them from their context, he can satisfy himself by referring to the original.

THE FIRST: 'How should Nature without Art make a great actor, since nothing happens on the stage exactly as in nature?' *Pollock, p. 5*

THE SECOND: Granted ; but no one has ever argued that Nature without Art, or sensibility without training, is sufficient to make a great actor, a good actor, or any sort of actor at all. The emotionalists to a man—Sainte-Albine, the nameless Englishman, and Sticotti—insist strongly on the need for technical accomplishment.

THE FIRST: 'What I require of a great actor is penetration and no sensibility ; the art of imitating everything, or, in other words, the same aptitude for every sort of character and part.' *Pollock, p. 7*

THE SECOND: No doubt the ideal actor (the unattainable ideal) is the man who has a perfect aptitude for every conceivable character—'a soft mass of sculptor's clay,' as M. Coquelin puts it, 'capable of assuming at will any form.' But what you have to prove is that the lack of sensibility in himself will assist him in imitating the manifestations of sensibility in his characters, and in affecting the sensibilities of his audience. *M. Coquelin, Harper's Magazine, lxxiv. p. 894*

THE FIRST: 'It is not in the stress of the first burst that characteristic traits present themselves. . . . He who comes upon the stage without having his whole action arranged and marked out will be a *Pollock, p. 12* *Pollock, p. 96* beginner all his life. Or if, endowed with intrepidity, confidence, and spirit, he relies on his quickness of wit and the habit of his calling, he will carry you away with his fire and fury, and you will applaud him as an expert in painting may smile at a free sketch where all is indicated and nothing defined.'

THE SECOND: Here we come upon one of the most frequent forms in which 'sensibility' is held to manifest itself—to wit, a tendency to rely on the inspiration of the moment. It is clear that, whether wise or unwise, this is possible only within very narrow limits. In any properly rehearsed play it can apply to nothing but facial expression, gesture, and tones of the voice ; or if to positions and 'business,' then only in scenes in which the player has the stage practically to himself. When two or more persons are playing together, their movements can no more be determined on the spur of the moment than can the movements of a watch-wheel. Each is part of a mechanism which the least lack of precision will put out of gear. Only among amateurs, or in the veriest 'scratch' performances, is this rule neglected, and then not from any trust in the virtues of sensibility, but simply from *Pollock,* bad stage-management. Diderot admirably states *p 27* the object of rehearsal to be' the striking of a balance between the different talents of the actors, so as to establish a general unity in the playing.' This is its final function ; but its first and more obvious purpose is merely to put each of the cog-wheels in its proper place. The watch must be pieced together before it can be regulated.

The details which it is possible to leave to inspiration are, doubtless, of vast importance, and, as we shall see, the practice of different actors in admitting or excluding the suggestions of the moment varies very widely.   But we shall also see that absolute pre-regulation of even the minutest gestures is quite consistent with genuine feeling—that is, with the presence in the actor's own organism of the physical symptoms of the emotion he is seeking to express. *Post, chap. xii.*

THE FIRST : ' These plaintive and sorrowful tones, drawn from the very depth of a mother's heart . . . are these not the result of true feeling ?   Are these not the very inspiration of despair ?   Not at all ; and the proof is that they are measured, that they form part of a system of declamation, that, raised or lowered by the twentieth part of a quarter of a tone, they ring false.'

THE SECOND : Precisely ; but is it not the skilful use of that delicate imaginative mechanism called ' sensibility' which enables the great actress to adjust her vocal cords to this subtle nicety of tone? *Post, p. 208*

THE FIRST : At the close of a performance ' The actor is tired, you are sad.   He has had exertion without feeling, you feeling without exertion.   Were it otherwise, the player's lot would be the most wretched on earth ; but he is not the person he represents ; he plays it, and plays it so well that you think he is the person ; the illusion is all on your side ; he knows well enough that he is not the person.' *Pollock, p. 17* *Post, p. 159*

THE SECOND : Another purely imaginary phase of sensibility—a tendency to become absolutely incarnate in your character, so as to undergo all his emotions in their fullest acuteness. Not even Sainte-Albine has argued that this is either advisable or possible; yet it is one of the absurdities which the anti-emotionalists are fondest of setting up and knocking down again. '"Are you, sir [Dr. Johnson asked John Philip Kemble], one of those enthusiasts who believe yourself transformed into the very character you represent?" Upon Mr. Kemble's answering that he had never felt so strong a persuasion himself; "To be sure not, sir (said Johnson;) the thing is impossible. And if Garrick really believed himself to be that monster, Richard the Third, he deserved to be hanged every time he performed it."'

Johnson and Kemble, Boswell, iv. p. 243

Diderot's psychology of the audience is surely as false as his psychology of the actor. Here Johnson was in advance of him. 'Nay, you know,' he said, 'nobody imagines that he [the player] is the character he represents. They say "See *Garrick*! how he looks to-night! See how he'll clutch the dagger!" That is the buz of the theatre.' There is no absolute illusion on either side. Salvini knows as well as the public, and the public knows as well as Salvini, that he is not Othello. Were it otherwise, we could no more endure to see the tragedy than he to act it. The emotionalist position is that both actor and audience should yield themselves up to the illusion to a certain extent; the anti-emotionalist position is that the actor will more easily and certainly beget illusion in the audience if he remains entirely free from it himself. These, I take it, are

Boswell, v. p. 46

the opposing theses. To disprove or ridicule a theory
which no one has advanced—a theory which implies
an absolute transmigration of soul from Richard to
Garrick, from Othello to Salvini—is to darken counsel   Salvini
by words without relevance. Salvini, indeed, uses the   *Post, p.* 145
word 'transmigration,' but he uses it in a figurative,
not in a literal and, so to speak, supernatural sense.

THE FIRST (emphatically): '*Extreme sensibility*   *Pollock,*
makes middling actors ; middling sensibility makes the   *p.* 17
ruck of bad actors ; a complete absence of sensibility
paves the way for the sublime actor.'

THE SECOND: This, at least, is explicit and precise. But beware, Monsieur le Premier! It is rash
for a disputant of your nimbleness to tether himself
to a dogma. The chain may gall you ere long.

THE FIRST: 'If this or that actor or actress were   *Pollock,*
as deeply moved as people imagine, do you suppose   *p.* 31
one would think of casting an eye round the boxes,
another of smiling to someone at the wing, and almost
all of speaking straight at the pit?[1] Do you suppose
that the call-boy would have to interrupt a hearty fit
of laughter in the green-room, to tell the laugher that
the time has come for him to go on and stab himself?'

THE SECOND: These, you tell me, are common
incidents of the player's calling? So be it. And they
indicate absence of sensibility? Quite so. Are we
to understand, then, that the majority of actors are
'sublime'? Even at the Théâtre-Français in 1770

---

[1] 'Parler au parterre.' I am not sure that this does not refer to the
practice of interrupting the play to address the audience, noticed in so
many anecdotes.

one would rather expect to find the majority 'middling' along with a fair percentage of the unmistakably 'bad.' Now middling actors, according to the
dogma, owe their mediocrity to 'extreme sensibility,'
while 'middling sensibility' is the bane of 'the ruck
of bad actors.' Hence it ensues that in any given
company two or three 'sublime' players at most
should be capable of giving the above-mentioned
proof of insensibility, while the majority should be
subject to those errors and weaknesses which arise
from sensibility, whether middling or extreme. In
short, the dogma and the argument do not dovetail.
One or other must be abandoned ; and, for my part, I
think the argument the fitter to survive. It is quite
true that many actors can recognise their friends in
the boxes ; quite true that many can indulge in bye-
play of all sorts, unnoticed (more or less) by the audience ; quite true that many a player has broken off a
burst of laughter in the green-room to go and give
himself the happy despatch on the stage. But of
these truths we have an obvious explanation, involving
no paradox. It is simply that the ruck of middling
and bad actors perform their parts mechanically,
not feeling, not even understanding them ; while, on
the other hand, there is no reason why actors who
feel, be they good, bad, or indifferent, should not at
the same time have all their wits about them.

Post, chap.
ix.

We shall find hereafter that many of the greatest
actors remain intent on their character throughout the
whole of a performance, even when absent from the
stage, and though not, of course, unconscious of their

audience, are neither able nor willing to distinguish individuals in front of the house. Sarah Siddons was one of these concentrated players ; Tommaso Salvini is another. According to the dogma, then, Siddons and Salvini should be, not the greatest in their respective spheres, but at best a pair of mediocrities. Is the dogma false ? Or is the world deluded ?

THE FIRST : ' When *Inès de Castro* was first performed, the pit burst out laughing at the point where the children appear. Mlle. Duclos, who played Inès, apostrophised the laughers indignantly : " Ris donc, sot parterre, au plus bel endroit de la pièce. . . ." Quinault-Dufresne plays the part of Severus in *Polyeucte*. Sent by the Emperor Decius to persecute the Christians, he confides to a friend his real feelings with regard to that calumniated sect. Common sense requires that this confidence . . . should be uttered in a low tone. The pit calls to him, " Plus haut ! " He replies to the pit, " Et vous, messieurs, plus bas ! " . . . Caillot is playing *Le Déserteur*. . . . At the very moment of his agony, when he is on the point of being dragged to execution, he notices that the chair on which he will have to lay down the fainting Louise is badly placed, and he rearranges it while singing in a moribund voice, " Mes yeux vont se fermer sans avoir vu Louise." [1] . . . Lekain, as Ninias, enters his father's tomb, and there cuts his mother's throat. He comes forth with blood-stained hands, horror-stricken, wild-eyed, quivering. . . . Yet seeing a diamond drop which has fallen from an actress's ear, he pushes it

Marginal notes:
Mrs. Siddons and Salvini
Post, pp. 139, 145
Pollock p. 46
Mlle. Duclos
Quinault-Dufresne
Caillot
Pollock, p. 87
Lekain
Pollock, p. 47

[1] Misquoted in the original.

with his foot towards the wing. And these actors
feel ? Impossible !'

THE SECOND : Concerning the first two anecdotes : is a sudden revulsion of feeling a phenomenon
undreamt of in your psychology? Even supposing
that to 'feel' a part necessarily implied a somnambulistic absorption in it (a quite gratuitous supposition),
can we not conceive Duclos and Quinault to have
been wakened from their trance by the interruptions
of the pit, and to have vented the irritability of 'the
sleeper awakened' in the first phrases that sprang to
their lips ? Their very audacity indicates that they
were not acting in cold blood, but were in a measure
beside themselves. As for Caillot and Lekain, their
actions afford simple instances of the manifold activity
of consciousness at any given moment. Why should
stage emotion be supposed to absorb all a man's faculties, when the most poignant emotion in real life does
nothing of the sort? On the contrary, it will often
Post, p. 161 sharpen our senses in every direction, producing, not
anæsthesia, but hyperæsthesia. We all know how
memory registers the smallest details of any scene
which has witnessed a crisis in our lives, as Fagin, in
the dock, 'counted the iron spikes before him, and
wondered how the head of one had been broken off,
and whether they would mend it or leave it as it
was.' We know how, even under the first shock of
a great catastrophe, men are often found to attend
with mechanical punctiliousness to the minutest trifles
of everyday existence. The man who has determined
to jump off Waterloo Bridge at midnight will wind

up his watch as usual at eleven o'clock ; and if he chance to see a sixpenny-piece on the pavement of Wellington Street, he will, in all probability, stoop and pick it up. The actual Ninias, had he found a jewel lying in his path, would probably have picked it up and put it in his pocket. Men led to execution have been known to be very particular about details of their dress, or to borrow an umbrella from the sheriff lest they should catch cold. Sir Thomas More jested with the headsman. Charles II., with the death-rattle in his throat, apologised to his courtiers for taking such an unconscionable time to die. All these persons may be presumed to have felt their situation deeply, and no situation can be more absorbing than that of a man in the jaws of death. We shall find many instances in the sequel of divided mental activity. In the meantime, I submit that Lekain's adroitness in saving the jewel does not prove him to have been insensible to the terror of the situation, any more than William Tell's dexterity in splitting the apple proves him to have been indifferent to the fate of his son.

No array of examples of presence of mind will practically further the anti-emotionalists' case. They should rather bring forward instances in which an actor's total absorption in his part ·has placed him at the mercy of accidents, and has thus injured the desired effect. These, unfortunately, are not so easily discovered. *Post, p.* 16

THE FIRST: ' A sure way to play in a petty, mean style, is to play your own character. Suppose you are a tartuffe, a miser, a misanthrope ; you may play the part well enough, but you will not come near the poet's creation ; for that is *the* Tartuffe, *the* Miser, *the* Misanthrope.'

THE SECOND : What has this to do with sensibility, in any conceivable sense of the term? Sensibility comes into play through imaginative sympathy ; and no one, however great a hypocrite or miser, can have any sort of sympathy with Tartuffe or Harpagon. Egoism is of the essence of evil. The hypocrite lives upon the uprightness of others, the miser upon their generosity ; and every additional hypocrite and miser is a victim the less and a competitor the more. They are not even influenced by the motives which induce felons to form offensive and defensive alliances. Each would like nothing better than to have a monopoly of his own vice. They are the Ishmaels of the social system. Vices of sensuality establish a freemasonry among their devotees, but hypocrisy and avarice serve only to isolate and harden.

A conscious hypocrite, even if it were possible that the triumphs and defeats of his patron saint should touch his 'sensibility,' would be the last to reveal the mysteries of his craft and of his soul by playing Tartuffe. To do so would be, not to assume, but to throw away, a mask; and his mask is his stock-in-trade. An unconscious hypocrite, if naturally unctuous in manner (which by no means follows), might have a peculiar facility for entering into the skin of Tartuffe. John Palmer, the first and perhaps the greatest Joseph Surface, was commonly

John
Palmer

known as 'Plausible Jack.' In a dispute with Sheridan, he began in his oily and rotund manner, ' If you could but see my heart, Mr. Sheridan ! ' when the playwright-manager cut him short with the remark, 'Why, Jack, you forget that I wrote it ! ' But Palmer's success in Joseph Surface had nothing to do with 'sensibility.' No one thinks of engaging a murderer to play Macbeth, not because his sensibility would lead him to act 'in a petty, mean style,' but because the very idea is an absurdity. To argue that Mr. Willard is not necessarily a villain because he plays the villain so well, or that his ' Spider ' would not be so good as it is were he himself a swell-mobsman, is simply to insult our intelligence. Only in the lowest stages of dramatic culture does anyone think of confounding the actor's ethics with those of his personage. There is a legend of a backwoodsman becoming so incensed with the villainy of Iago that he drew his revolver and shot, or shot at, the actor. It is said, too, that Provost, who played Napoleon's gaoler, Sir Hudson Lowe, at the Porte Saint-Martin, had to be escorted home from the theatre lest the infuriated gods should fall upon him and lynch him. These savages of the backwoods or the boulevards are the persons who require to have it proved to them that a hypocrite will not make the best Tartuffe or a miser the best Harpagon. The old lady who left Edmund Kean a handsome legacy on seeing his Othello, and revoked it after his performance of the contemptible Luke in Massinger's *City Madam*, might also have learnt something from Diderot's argument.

Dorar, iii. p. 142

Provost, *Coquelin, p.* 30

Hawkins, i. p. 259

D

Whether a lover will make the best Romeo is another and somewhat more rational question, to be *Post, p. 92* considered hereafter.

I shall not dispute Diderot's demonstration of the inconveniences of too much sensibility in private life. It is scarcely to the purpose ; for the idiosyncracy which makes a man stammer and hesitate in improvising a declaration of love on his own account, may be the very thing to aid him in lending fervour and conviction to a mimic declaration, the words of which are supplied by Shakespeare or Alfred de Musset. Neither do I insist upon the fact, which Diderot's actor-disciples should lay to heart, that his theory is *Pollock,* based upon a hearty contempt for their calling. 'In *p. 63* society,' he says, 'unless they are buffoons, I find actors polished, caustic, cold, proud, dissipated, profuse, selfish, alive to our absurdities rather than touched by our misfortunes ; unmoved at the sight of a melancholy incident or at the recital of a pathetic story ; pariahs, vagabonds, slaves of the great ; without conduct, without friends, without any of the holy and tender ties which associate us in the pains and pleasures of another, who in turn shares our own. I have often seen an actor laugh off the stage, I do not remember to have seen one weep. What do they do, then, with the sensibility they arrogate, and are supposed to possess ? Do they leave it on the stage at their exit to take it up again at their next entrance ?' Here we have again the contradiction pointed out above. If this be a fair description of actors in general, what comes of the dogma that extreme sensibility makes middling actors and middling sensibility the ruck of bad actors? We are now assured that actors as a class are devoid of sensibility; how comes it, then, that actors as a class are not 'sublime'? This, however, is not essential. Diderot's theory may be right though his arguments are inconsistent. What I have sought to show is that his reasoning breaks down, or at least straggles off and loses itself, for lack of a definition of terms. He does not know clearly either what he himself is maintaining, or what he is arguing against. He is proving, half the time, that sensibility is mischievous, while the other half he devotes to showing that it does not exist.

We have seen that he attributes to sensibility four leading phases :—

i. A tendency to do without study and to rely on momentary inspiration.

ii. A tendency to become incarnate in your personage, to live in it and in it alone, to feel all its emotions and endure all its agonies.

iii. A tendency to somnambulistic absorption in the business of the scene, making consciousness for the moment one and indivisible.

iv. A tendency to express your own moral nature, instead of assuming and exhibiting the character created by the playwright.

At last, however, in a rash moment, Diderot is actually betrayed into defining 'sensibility,' and at once the debate is practically at an end. 'Sensibility,' *Pollock, p. 56* so the definition runs, '. . . is that disposition which accompanies organic weakness, mobility of the diaphragm, vivacity of the imagination, delicacy of the nerves, which inclines one to . . . loss of self-control, to exaggeration, to contempt, to disdain, to obtuseness to the true, the good, and the beautiful, to injustice, to madness.' Sensibility, then, is a morbid habit of mind and body, which must interfere, not with acting alone, but with all healthy art whatsoever. This is self-evident. Any criticism of such a conclusion is futile. But how about the definition? Supposing such a multitude of effects—I have only quoted half of them—to arise from one cause, can we fairly call that cause sensibility? Hysteria, surely, is a much apter name for the disease. Substituting this term, then, we read Diderot's thesis as follows :—' The great actor must not be hysterical.' Agreed. But where is the paradox?

Nineteenth
Century,
ix. p. 695
' Ne lui demandez pas,' says M. Paul Janet of Diderot, ' des œuvres méditées, composées avec art, écrites avec goût, liées dans toutes leurs parties. . . . Ce ne sont jamais que des fragments, des lueurs éclatantes, mais passagères, d'admirables improvisations : mais tout ce qui est raisonnement suivi, liaison d'idées, enchaînement systématique de propositions, enfin construction régulière et équilibrée, est chose inconnue pour cet esprit fumeux où tout est sans cesse à l'état de bouillonnement et de fermentation.'

CHAPTER IV.

'SUNT LACRYMÆ RERUM.'

THE first two sections of my interrogatory are, I think, the most essential. They take us to the very kernel of the matter.

There are certain simple emotions which tend to express themselves directly and unmistakably in changes of the physical organs. The chief of these are grief and joy (with all their subdivisions), rage, terror, and shame. The more complex emotions have no such proper and instant symptoms. Love and hatred, jealousy and envy, for example, are rather attitudes of mind than individual emotions. They may have their appropriate facial expressions, but a very slight effort of will suffices to smooth even these away ; whereas we all know how hard it is to repress the physical manifestations of grief or terror. The complex and, so to speak, habitual emotions utter themselves from time to time through the medium of the simple emotions. Love, it is needless to say, will run the whole gamut of grief and joy ; hatred, in the presence of the hated object, will burst forth in the form of rage. Thus the physical effects of the simple emotions may be regarded as the raw material of expression ; whence it follows that the reproduction of these physical effects must be the very groundwork of the actor's art. And of the simple emotions, grief in all its phases is, to the actor, by far the most important. I do not mean that life is a vale of tears, and that the stage, in holding as 'twere the mirror up to nature, must therefore be more intimately con- cerned with weeping than with laughter. Something might be said for this view of the matter, but I do not intend to say it. What I mean is that, with the exception of terror, which is of comparatively rare occurrence, no emotion manifests itself so directly, so inevitably, and so peculiarly as grief. Joy is much more easily repressed, and much more various in its symptoms ; therefore it calls for less absolute fidelity of imitation. We take it for granted much more readily than grief. Great joy, indeed, will often bor- row its expression from grief, but not so grief from joy, unless it passes over into positive madness. To look at the matter from another point of view, do we not see that from the days of Thespis downwards the gift of pathos has been regarded as the actor's highest endowment, the representation of pity, sorrow, and despair as his worthiest task ? It is often said that every low comedian aspires to play Macbeth ; in other words, everyone instinctively recognises that it is a much simpler and more trivial task to make the un- skilful laugh than to make the judicious grieve. Some years ago, on the occasion of one of Mr. Toole's numerous appearances in the witness-box, the judge, intending a compliment, maladroitly remarked that

he was sure no one had ever wept while Mr. Toole
was on the stage. 'I am very sorry to hear it, my
lord' was the comedian's reply ; and indeed his lord-
ship's pleasantry showed a strange ignorance not only
of human nature in general but of Mr. Toole's art in
particular. To sum the matter up, then, the rendering
of grief and its kindred shades of emotion is univer-
sally accepted as the highest problem of the actor's
craft ; and the question, 'How may this rendering
be best effected ?' is the central point of the whole
discussion.

Mr. Toole

There is no doubt that the imagination can in
some cases so act on the physical organism as to produce in a more or less acute degree the characteristic
symptoms of grief ; while, on the other hand, these
symptoms may to some extent be imitated by the
direct action of the will upon the muscles, with little
or no aid from the imagination. Which method is
the better calculated to work on the sympathies of a
theatrical audience ? 'The latter,' say Diderot and his
adherents ; 'The former,' his adversaries retort. I
have tried, therefore, to ascertain, first, whether the
tendency of the imagination to act on the lachrymal
glands and the muscles of the throat is general or
exceptional ; secondly, whether the actors in whom
this tendency exists have found it help or hinder their
efforts to speak to the hearts of their hearers. For
this, I need scarcely say, is the one ultimate test.
Whatever may be the case with the other arts, its
immediate effect upon the average audience is the
be-all and end-all of acting. Nothing is absolutely

right or wrong, artistic or inartistic. If real tears
help to move the average audience, they are right and
artistic ; if they tend to cast a damp over the house,
they are inartistic and wrong.

My first question, then, was this :—

In moving situations, do tears come to your eyes ? Do they
come unbidden ? Can you call them up and repress them at
will ? In delivering pathetic speeches does your voice break of
its own accord ? Or do you deliberately simulate a broken voice ?
Supposing that, in the same situation, you on one night shed
real tears and speak with a genuine 'lump in your throat,' and
on the next night simulate these affections without physically
experiencing them : on which occasion should you expect to
produce the greater effect upon your audience ?

All testimony, old and new, agrees in asserting
that, whatever their artistic value, real tears are
habitually and copiously shed upon the stage. The
ancients are at one both as to their reality and as to
their artistic value. Hackneyed though it be, the in-
evitable passage from Horace must lead the way :—

Horace

*Ars
Poetica,
l.* 101-103

Ut ridentibus adrident, ita flentibus adsunt [1]
Humani vultus. Si vis me flere, dolendum est
Primum ipsi tibi ; tunc tua me infortunia lædent.

*Coning-
ton's trans.*
(1870)

Smiles are contagious ; so are tears ; to see
Another sobbing, brings a sob from me.
No, no, good Peleus ; set the example, pray,
And weep yourself, then weep perhaps I may.

Some critics have maintained that the maxim
is not addressed to actors but to tragic poets. If so,
Horace has certainly expressed himself with less than

[1] Or 'adflent.'

Horatian lucidity ; and there can be little doubt that even if he had not the stage actually in his mind, he would without hesitation have extended the principle to mimetic art.

The orators are still more emphatic ; and oratory is sufficiently analogous to acting to give their opinions great weight. Judging by mere antecedent probability, one would not be surprised to find them in the anti-emotionalist camp. However important self-control may be to the actor, it must be doubly so to the forensic orator. If, then, the symptoms of emotion, physically experienced, are inconsistent with perfect self-control, one would expect to find Cicero and Quintilian insisting on absolute insensibility. The fact that their precepts take the opposite direction seems to show that the clouding of the eyes does not necessarily involve the clouding of the brain.

First let us hear Cicero :—' Nor is it possible,' he says, ' for the hearer to grieve, or hate, or fear, or to be moved to commiseration and tears, unless the emotions which the speaker wishes to communicate are deeply impressed upon himself, and stamped on his own bosom in characters of fire. . . . Never, I assure you, have I endeavoured to excite in the judges the emotions of grief, commiseration, envy or hatred, without becoming sensibly touched myself with the passions I wished to communicate to them. . . . And do not suppose it something extraordinary and wonderful for the speaker to be so often subjected to the violent excitement of grief, and anger, and every other passion of the mind, especially in the interests of strangers ;

Cicero, *De Oratore, ii.* 45, 46 (*Calvert's trans.*)

for there is an emotional power in the sentiments and
topics themselves which supersedes the necessity of all
simulation and falsehood. . . . What can be more
unreal than poetry, than fable, than the creations of
the drama? Yet often in this fictitious scene I have
marked the eyes of the actor flashing fire through his
mask when declaiming these lines :—

> What ! did you then dare to spurn him from you?
> Or to enter Salamis without him?
> Did you not dread the aspect of his father?

. . . Then subduing his voice to the tone of commiseration, he proceeded mournfully, and in seeming
tears :—

> Whom, in extremest age and penury,
> You cruelly have lacerated, robbed
> Of children, and of life, regardless of
> Your brother's death, regardless of the child,
> The little child committed to your charge.

If the actor who had to declaim these verses daily
could not do so effectually without an emotion of
sorrow, can you suppose that Pacuvius himself, when
composing them, was in an indifferent and listless
state of mind?' The phrase 'flens et lugens dicere
videbatur,' here translated 'he proceeded mournfully
and in seeming tears,' does not appear to me to bear
quite that interpretation. The word 'seeming' con-
flicts with the general tenor of the passage; better
Latinists than I must determine whether the incon-
sistency is due to Cicero or to his translator.

Quintilian   Quintilian, again, is very explicit on the subject of
stage tears, while he speaks with no less conviction than
Cicero of the rhetorical value of emotion physically

experienced : —' The great secret . . . for moving the
passions is to be moved ourselves ; for the imitation of
grief, anger, indignation, will often be ridiculous, if our
words and countenance alone conform to the emotion,
not our heart. . . . Wherefore, when we wish to attain
verisimilitude in emotion, let us put ourselves in the
place of those who really suffer ; and let our speech
proceed from the very state of mind which we wish
to induce in the judge. Will he grieve who hears
me declaim unmoved ? . . . Will he weep who sees
me dry-eyed ? . . . But how shall we be affected, our
emotions not being at our command ? This, too, I
shall try to explain. What the Greeks call φαντασίας,
we call *visiones* ; whereby the images of things absent
are so represented to the mind, that we seem to see
them with our eyes, and to have them present before
us. Whoever shall have conceived these thoroughly,
will have complete power over his emotions. . . . I
have often seen histrions and actors, on laying aside
their masks after some mournful scene, continue to
shed tears. If, then, the mere pronouncing of another's
words can thus beget unreal emotions, what should
not we effect, who ought to think our own words, and
to be moved on behalf of our clients ? . . . I have
often been moved, not only to tears, but to pallor and
every symptom of grief.'

The often-cited anecdotes of Polus and Æsopus
will come in at a later stage of our inquiry. For the
present, I need only note that these passages from
Cicero and Quintilian seem to represent the general
opinion of the antique world upon mimetic tears and

*De Institu-
tione Ora-
toria, vi. 2*

*Post, pp.
78, 167*

their value.   I do not pretend to have ransacked the classics for utterances on the subject, but we are justified in supposing, I think, that if any Greek or Roman had anticipated Diderot, the anti-emotionalists would not have failed, long ere this, to appeal in triumph to his authority.   For my part, I lay no great stress on the evidence of antiquity.   The conditions of acting, and even of oratory, have altered too much to justify us in accepting as infallible the maxims of classic theorists.   The passages quoted above prove that real tears were habitually shed on the antique scene, and that Cicero and Quintilian believed in their artistic value.   I do not allege that their authority is conclusive.   We cannot receive with blind humility the doctrines in vogue in a city where the theatre was overtowered by the amphitheatre.

Shakespeare, Hamlet, ii. 2, and iii. 2

Shakespeare's utterances on the subject of mimetic emotion are familiar to everyone.   As I have said before, they seem to me to sum up the subject, and as my argument proceeds I shall have to quote them for the ten-thousandth time.   For the present, I need only mention them to recall their purport, at any rate, to the reader's memory.

The records of the stage, it may almost be said, are tear-stained on every page.   We have ample and unquestionable evidence that many of the greatest artists frequently, if not habitually, wept in pathetic situations.   To go at once to the greatest of all, we

Garrick and Mrs. Cibber, Davies, iii. p. 75

read in Tom Davies, who had the best opportunities for observation, that ' In some very affecting scenes, Garrick and Mrs. Cibber have worked themselves up to the shedding of tears, especially in the parts of Lear and Cordelia.' Garrick's most formidable rival was Spranger Barry, and the part in which their rivalry culminated was Romeo. Here is the account of Barry's death-scene given by that excellent critic the anonymous author of *The Actor* : ' His sensibility gets the better of his articulation ; his grief takes effect upon the organs of his voice ; and the very tone of it is altered : it is broken, hoarse, and indistinct. We give the applause to this consummate piece of playing that it deserves : we see nature triumphing over what art would direct ; and we give it a praise which art, without this strong appearance of nature, never could deserve.' Charles Reade, if we may believe the same writer, was justified in making the famous tear roll down Peg Woffington's cheek. ' Mrs. Woffington,' he says, ' has great sensibility ; and she has, more than most players of either sex, given a loose to nature in the expressing it ; to this she owed the greatest part of her fame as an actress ; and in this she always excelled, when her private passions did not interfere.' Garrick's famous criticism of Mrs. Pritchard, whose commanding genius is attested by Churchill and Johnson, among a host of lesser critics, shows that she not only wept, but wept immoderately. ' Her scenes of grief were tiresomely blubbering,' he said to Tate Wilkinson. As for Mrs. Siddons, though she belonged to a school we should not have been surprised to find dry-eyed, we have her own testimony to the 'bitter tears of rage, disappointment, betrayed confidence, and baffled ambition ' which ' gushed into

[Marginal notes:]

Barry

Ed. 1755, *p.* 56

Peg Woffington, *Ed.* 1755, *p.* 105

Mrs. Pritchard, *Wilkinson,* i. *p.* 140

Mrs. Siddons

Post, p. 139

her eyes' in the part of Constance—one of her very

Crabb
Robinson,
iii. p. 19

greatest. Fanny Kelly, in her 'Dramatic Recollec-
tions' (a sort of lecture which she used to deliver),
related that when, as a child, she played Arthur in
King John, 'her collar was wet with Mrs. Siddons'
tears.' Mr. Siddons, it may be added, took an irre-

Dibdin,
p. 190

verently prosaic view of his wife's emotion. 'Do you
know,' he said to the Rev. Dr. Mackenzie, minister
of Portpatrick, 'that small beer is good for crying?
The day that my wife drinks small beer, she cries
amazingly ; she is really pitiful. But if I was to give
her porter, or any stronger liquor, she would not be
worth a farthing.' It is to be feared that Mr. Siddons
was indulging in a joke at the expense of his clerical
friend.

Fanny
Kemble

        Fanny Kemble, if not so great an actress as her
aunt, was a keen observer. She bears witness to the

Post, p. 151

reality of her own tears in a passage to be quoted in
another place. Still more interesting is her account of

Miss
O'Neill
Réflexions
sur Lekain,
p. 56

the emotional idiosyncracy of Miss O'Neill, that living
embodiment of womanly pathos, who, according to
Talma, drew tears from Frenchmen who knew no
English by the mere magic of her voice. 'She had a
rare endowment for her especial range of characters,'

Record of a
Girlhood,
ii. p. 20

says Fanny Kemble, 'in an easily excited superficial
sensibility, which caused her to cry, as she once said to
me, "buckets full," and enabled her to exercise the (to
most men) irresistible influence of a beautiful woman in
tears. The power (or weakness) of abundant weeping
without disfigurement is an attribute of deficient rather
than excessive feeling. In such persons the tears are

poured from their crystal cups without muscular distortion of the rest of the face. In proportion to the violence or depth of emotion, and the acute or profound sensibility of the temperament, is the disturbance of the countenance. In sensitive organisations, the muscles round the nostrils and lips quiver and are distorted, the throat and temples swell, and a grimace, which but for its miserable significance would be grotesque, convulses the whole face. . . . Women of the temperament I have alluded to above, have fountains of lovely tears behind their lovely eyes, and their weeping, which is indescribably beautiful, is comparatively painless, and yet pathetic enough to challenge tender compassion.' In this very curious analysis there is no doubt a great deal of justice. It is particularly interesting in its bearing upon the quantitative relation (so to speak) of mimetic to real *Post, p. 201* emotion.

In French dramatic records there is sometimes a difficulty in distinguishing between the figurative and the literal use of the word 'larmes.' A critic will often talk of an actor's 'larmes' when he is evidently thinking merely of his pathetic power in general, and does not mean expressly to affirm that at any given moment he shed actual tears. I have come across many instances, however, in which there is no ambiguity. Of the great actress, for example, *Mlle. Champmeslé* who was trained by Racine to create the chief of his heroines, Lemazurier writes as follows :—'Il n'était *Lemazurier, ii. p. 72* pas nécessaire de répéter à Mad. Champmeslé ce précepte de Boileau,

Il faut dans la douleur, que vous vous abaissiez ;
Pour m'arracher des pleurs, il faut que vous pleuriez.

Sa sensibilité était naturelle et vraie ; quelque force
d'esprit que l'on eût, quelque violence que l'on se fît,
il fallait partager sa douleur, et pleurer avec elle.'
Lemazurier, it is true, could not speak as an eye-
witness, but he was a careful writer who would not
have expressed himself thus explicitly without good
authority. Dorat, on the other hand, wrote as an
eye-witness of Duclos, Adrienne Lecouvreur's chief
rival :—' Ses larmes étoient belles, sa douleur tou-
chante, sa figure vraiment tragique : elle pleuroit à
tort et à travers ; mais enfin elle pleuroit, et c'en étoit
assez pour émouvoir le Spectateur.' Sticotti, in a note
to his *Garrick*, declares that ' *Dufrêne, la Gaussin,
Mlle. Q[uinault*] jouant la sœur du *Glorieux*, versoient
des pleurs ; notre ame reconnoissante se plaît encore
à s'en retracer les charmes.' Quinault-Dufresne was
the greatest actor of his time, the French Quin ; Mlle.
Gaussin was the original Zaïre ; and Mlle. Quinault
was one of the most famous members of a famous
family. Rachel, I suspect, was apt to have more fire
than moisture in her eyes. It is related that on her
death-bed she told her sister Sarah that she had
been thinking over and trying to elaborate the part
of Pauline in *Polyeucte*, adding pathetically, ' Pour
étudier il faut penser et pleurer, mais je ne vois plus
que des fantômes qui fuient.' This is sufficient to
prove that she was by no means the emotionless
creature who, according to Diderot, has alone the
right to be ' sublime ' ; but tears shed in study or

*Mlle.
Duclos
Dorat,
Préface,
p. 17*

*Ed. 1770,
p. 149*

Rachel

*Houssaye,
p. 335*

rehearsal are not the same thing as tears shed in the moment of the performance. Frédérick Lemaître, with all his faults, was undoubtedly one of the greatest of great actors, and of him Victor Hugo wrote, in a note on *Ruy Blas* : ' Et puis, partout, à travers les éclairs éblouissants de son jeu, M. Frédérick a des larmes, de ces vraies larmes qui font pleurer les autres, de ces larmes dont parle Horace : F. Lemaître

> Si vis me flere, dolendum est
> Primum ipsi tibi ; '

and Frédérick himself mentions, among the great qualities of his comrade Madame Dorval, ' ses larmes qui débordaient réellement du cœur.' Madame Dorval, *Souvenirs,* *p.* 99

Adelaide Neilson, I am assured by several observers, used to weep profusely both at rehearsal and during performance. Charlotte Cushman was not a woman one would suppose inclined to the melting mood ; yet her biographer, Mrs. Clement, says of her performance of Mrs. Haller in *The Stranger*, ' So much did Miss Cushman herself enter into the spirit of the part, that I have, on more than one occasion, seen Miss Neilson Miss Cushman *Charlotte Cushman,* *p.* 166

> Cadent tears fret channels in her cheeks.'

Mr. Toole in his recently published *Reminiscences* says of Benjamin Webster, the creator of Triplet : ' His Luke Fielding in *The Willow Copse* was full of his peculiar genius for domestic drama. It had one scene that was pathetic in the extreme. I have cried at it myself, and I never knew him play it without the tears streaming down his cheeks. It is the scene where the supposed dishonour of his B. Webster

E

daughter is made manifest to him. " Come with me, we have no longer a place among the honest and the good," were, I think, the words which take him off from among the neighbours and friends before whom the disgrace of his child had been pronounced.'

I pass now to the observations and experiences of living artists. Among those who are in the habit of playing pathetic parts the proclivity to tears is almost universal. As to their precise artistic value, opinions are a good deal divided ; but I find no one in whom they tend to arise asserting that they should be altogether repressed. It is upon the question how far they may safely be indulged without endangering self-control that authorities differ. Almost everyone admits that at the commencement of his stage career (the stiff frigidity of the amateur being once over-come) the emotion of a part has often tended to run away with him ; but I can find no case in which this has been corrected by a deliberate effort to eradicate the habit of feeling. It has simply been left to ex-perience and practice to establish that due balance of the faculties which begets a temperance in the very torrent, tempest, and whirlwind of passion.

As I gave precedence to David Garrick among the actors of the past, no one will wonder to find me place Tommaso Salvini in the post of honour among living artists. To attempt any ' order of merit ' among my other informants would be invidious and absurd ; but Salvini's world-wide reputation entitles him to a priority which will scarcely be contested.

He delivers himself with no less emphasis than

Salvini

authority. 'If you do not weep in the agony of grief,' he writes, 'if you do not blush with shame, if you do not glow with love, if you do not tremble with terror, if your eyes do not become bloodshot with rage, if, in short, you yourself do not intimately experience whatever befits the diverse characters and passions you represent, you can never thoroughly transfuse into the hearts of your audience the sentiment of the situation.' Such an utterance from such an actor is of itself sufficient to prove that the anti-emotionalist theory, whatever truth it may contain, is not of universal application. The actor who is by constitution or conviction a disciple of Diderot may produce very great effects, but it is certain that some, at least, of the sublimest possibilities of theatrical art can be achieved by an actor who utterly rejects the philosopher's doctrine.

As a corollary to Salvini's dictum, let me quote an anecdote which he related to me during his last visit to London (February 1884). It occurred in the course of a conversation on the subject of the *Paradoxe*. 'See, I shall tell you a story,' he said. 'In *La Morte Civile* I always weep, and greatly. Now, there is in Rio Janeiro a newspaper editor, Senhor de Castro, a big, bearded man, with gold spectacles—proprio un' uomo serio!—who is famous for his lack of feeling. They say he buried his wife without a tear—I do not know, but they say so. He saw *La Morte Civile*, and after the curtain fell he came upon the stage. Behold! on each side of his nose there was a great wet furrow, and as he laid his hand upon my shoulder I could feel that it was twitching and trembling. And next day every one in Rio Janeiro went about saying : " He has made De Castro weep ! What a triumph ! " ' Then Salvini added : ' As to French tragedy, however, I can understand Diderot's theory. I now rarely appear in it. Orosmane is as a ghost after Othello.'

Mrs. Bancroft

'The performance of a moving situation,' Mrs. Bancroft writes, ' without the true ring of sensibility in the actor, must fail to affect any one. . . . An emotional break in the voice must be brought about naturally, and by a true appreciation of the sentiment, or what does it become ? I can only compare it to a bell with a wooden tongue—it makes a sound, but there it ends. I cannot simulate suffering without an honest sympathy with it. . . . I hold that without great nervous sensibility no one can act pathos. . . . It is impossible to feel the sentiments one has to utter, and but half the author's meaning can be conveyed. It is a casket with the jewel absent. . . . The voice in emotion must be prompted by the heart ; and if that is " out of tune and harsh," why, then, indeed, the voice is " like sweet bells jangled." Art *should* help nature, but nature *must* help art. They are twin sisters, and should go hand in hand, but nature must be the firstborn. I was once much impressed by a small child's criticism. He watched for a long time silently and attentively a scene of great emotional interest between two people. When asked what he thought of it, he answered, " I like that one best." " Why ? " " She speaks like telling the truth, and the other speaks like telling lies." What criticism can be finer than this? One was acting straight from the heart, the other from not even next door but one to it.' To give this anecdote its full value we should of course have positive evidence that the one was in tears, the other dry-eyed and unmoved. For obvious reasons such evidence is unattainable ; but Mrs. Bancroft, watching the scene doubtless from close at hand, and certainly with the keen eye of a mistress of the craft, is a scarcely less trustworthy witness than the artists themselves. Mr. Bancroft fully agrees with his accomplished wife as to the advantage possessed by an actor whose nerves and muscles sensitively respond to the touch of his imagination ; and no one who has seen Mr. Bancroft's irresistibly pathetic performance of Triplet will hesitate to admit that he speaks with authority. He adds that any counter-irritant which tends to dissipate the energy of the imagination is certain to interfere with the effect. For instance, he avows that amid the excitement of his farewell performance at the Haymarket he could not enter so thoroughly into the part of Triplet as to do himself full justice.

Mr. Bancroft

Mr. and Mrs. Kendal are strongly of opinion that the emotional effect they produce upon their audience varies in accordance with the greater or less emotional effect experienced by them in their own persons. The difference between parts they like and parts they do not like is that in the former they fall easily and naturally under the sway of the appropriate emotion, while in the latter they have to work them-

Mr. and Mrs. Kendal

selves up to it. ' We should all be great artists,' says
Mrs. Kendal, ' if we could choose each night the part
we feel in a humour for.' Could anything contradict more flatly the theory of the musical-box actor
who, having once wound himself up, can switch on at
will any tune in his whole repertory, and reel it off
without missing the twang of a single note? Mrs.
Kendal confesses herself very prone to tears on the
stage, even to the detriment of her make-up. She
mentions as an instance of the kind of speech which
she can never utter without real tears and a very real
break in the voice, that saying of Kate Verity in *The
Squire*, where she burns the relics of Thorndyke's
courtship, and holds her hands to the flame : ' A
lucky thing that Christie made such a bright fire for
me—(*shivering*)—and yet it's cold. Ah, I suppose
heat never comes from burnt love-letters.' No one
who remembers this play will contend that Mrs.
Kendal's emotion failed to move the audience.

   This is perhaps the fittest place in which to
quote some suggestive remarks on the value of stage-
tears by a critic I greatly esteem :—' An obtrusively
lachrymose performance,' he writes, 'tends to shock
rather than to move me, and I think most people
would say the same. It is such emotion as is not
expressed by tears and sobs—shame, despair, pity—
or even the exquisite expression of a quite opposite
order of emotion—wonder, love pure and simple, or
even joy—that brings tears to my eyes and sends
cold shivers down my spine. For example, in the

second act of *The Squire* there was much emotion
that could be expressed only by sobs and tears, and
was so expressed by Mrs. Kendal, most admirably ;
yet the two moments of the play that have remained
in my memory and will always remain there are
(1) Kate Verity's confession to Thorndyke in the first
act ' [the confession which causes Thorndyke, when
left alone on the stage, to drink ' Baby's health !'
—in milk] ' and (2) her sinking into a chair in Act
III. exclaiming " All the troubles of all the world
upon one little head "—in neither of which is the
emotion one that could possibly be expressed by the
signs you choose.' There is much truth in this
criticism. I am inclined to think that the actual
shedding of tears is not, in itself, particularly effective, and that we Anglo-Saxons of this generation
are perhaps less apt than our ancestors and ances-
tresses—less apt, too, than some of our continental
neighbours—to be moved by the ' summer tempest '
of sorrow. My correspondent goes too far in arguing that mere sobs and tears are never moving.
In a naturally pathetic situation which, in Bottom's
phrase, ' asks some tears in the true performing of it,'
a woman's weeping, even though it be of the convulsive kind described by Fanny Kemble, will always
give the sorrow its crown of sorrow. If my correspondent was unmoved by Mrs. Kendal's tears in the
third act of *The Squire*, that may have been owing to
what I take to be the essential falsity of much of the
sentiment in that particular scene. As a general rule,
however, unrestrained weeping is a mark of passivity,

whereas it is activity in one form or another that
most deeply interests and moves us. One of the
most touching of all phases of activity is the successful repression of tears. Triplet's exit speech, for
example, in the first act of *Masks and Faces* would
be ruined by the overflow of even a single tear-
drop. 'Madam,' he says, 'you have inspired a son of
Thespis with dreams of eloquence ; you have tuned to
a higher key a poet's lyre ; you have tinged a painter's
existence with brighter colours ; and—and——God
in heaven bless you, Margaret Woffington.' This
should clearly be spoken with a tremor of the voice
and a quiver of the lip, showing that tears are
near the surface and are only restrained by the poor
fellow's sense of manly dignity. Similar cases could
be cited in hundreds. They swarm in Shakespeare.
The best instance of all, perhaps, is that wonderful
snatch of dialogue in the fourth act of *Julius Cæsar* :

> *Cassius.* Of your philosophy you make no use,
> If you give place to accidental evils.
> *Brutus.* No man bears sorrow better :—Portia is dead.
> *Cassius.* Ha ! Portia !
> *Brutus.*   She is dead.
> *Cassius.* How 'scaped I killing when I crossed you so ? . . .
> *Brutus.* . . . With this she fell distract,
> And, her attendants absent, swallowed fire.
> *Cassius.* And died so ?
> *Brutus.*   Even so.
> *Cassius.*   O ye immortal gods !

Here, of course, the effort of repression can be simulated in cold-blood ; but, if my observation does not
mislead me, it is precisely in such passages that the

ear most quickly detects and rejects even the most delicate art of the mechanical performer.

Again, there is a distinction to be drawn between emotion belonging strictly to the character and emotion which comes, as it were, from outside. The player is both a participator in the action and a spectator. He looks before and after; he cannot divest his mind of a knowledge of the past and future; the irony of things, which is, by hypothesis, concealed from the personage he represents, is patent to him. Thus many speeches which, to the character uttering them, seem unemotional and even insignificant, are in the eyes of the audience and of the player charged with pathetic meaning. There is a famous instance in Racine's *Iphigénie en Aulide*, where Iphigénie, little dreaming of her doom, questions her father as to the pompous sacrifice which Calchas is preparing :—

Iphigénie. Verra-t-on à l'autel votre heureuse famille ?
Agamemnon. Hélas !
Iphigénie. Vous vous taisez !
Agamemnon. Vous y serez, ma fille.

Act ii. 2

Nay more, the mere literary perfection of a speech may give it, for some natures, a moving quality. For example, there are many passages in Chaucer, Wordsworth, Tennyson, and other poets—passages of no particular emotional significance—which I, for my part, would not undertake to read aloud without a tremor of the voice and an unwonted moisture of the eye. Actors as a class, I suspect, are not keenly susceptible to this form of emotional influence, but there must be cases in which it makes itself felt. In

the part of Minnie Gilfillian in *Sweet Lavender* Mr.
Pinero has placed several of those speeches which
seem to me to acquire an emotional quality from their
mere verbal charm.   For example :—

Minnie. But, Clem dear, I wish you'd do something to
please me.
Clement (*seizing her hands*).   I'll do anything.
Minnie. Anything but marry me.   (*Seriously*) Well, don't
wait for Uncle Geoffrey's return, but write to him, to Paris, and
tell him how you adore—my hated rival.   Uncle Geoff is a
bachelor, but married men and bachelors are manufactured
by the same process —Love, Clem—and he'll understand.   Tell
him all, and say that the girl you have lost your treacherous
heart to has won one staunch friend—Minnie Gilfillian.

Another instance, to compare great things with
small, is Gretchen's soliloquy in *Faust* :—

Du lieber Gott ! was so ein Mann
Nicht alles, alles denken kann !
Beschämt nur steh' ich vor ihm da,
Und sag' zu allen Sachen ja.
Bin doch ein arm unwissend Kind,
Begreife nicht was er an mir find't.

It would clearly be wrong for Iphigénie, or Minnie
Gilfillian, or Gretchen to bedew these speeches with
tears ; but I conceive that sensitiveness to such ex-
traneous emotional stirrings would have to be quite
abnormal before it could injuriously affect an artist's
performance.   In many declamatory passages it might
impart a vibration to the voice, the effect of which
could only be for good.

Much more might be said of this distinction between what may be called intrinsic and extrinsic feeling

—the feeling to which an actor is subject in so far as he is identified with his character, and the feeling to which he is subject precisely because such identification is necessarily incomplete. One form of extrinsic feeling which must of course be overcome is the awe with which great actors have been known to inspire their fellow-performers, to such a pitch as to destroy their self-mastery. Charles Young, Macready, and even the great John Philip himself, confess to having been so overcome by the acting of Mrs. Siddons as to be unable for the moment to carry on the business of the scene. 'Would you not, Sir,' said Boswell to Johnson, 'start as Mr. Garrick does, if you saw a ghost?' 'I hope not,' replied Johnson ; 'if I did, I should frighten the ghost.'. If the majesty of buried Denmark was ever 'frighted from his propriety' by the acting of his son, that emotion was evidently not only extrinsic but very much out of place. I fear, however, that the players of to-day are but little exposed to this danger.

Young, *Campbell,* *i. p.* 205
Macready, *Remi-niscences,* *i. p.* 54
Kemble, *Boswell,* *iv. p.* 243
Boswell, *v. p.* 38

'I shed tears on the stage every night when my " personage " weeps,' says Madame Sarah Bernhardt. 'Tears always come to my eyes,' writes Miss Geneviève Ward, 'in a moving situation, but seldom run over. Sometimes they are unbidden, and sometimes I work up to them. I have been obliged when studying a part (Constance in *King John*, for instance) to stop owing to the tears and sobs, and would not have attempted to play it until I could control my feelings. I find that I feel much more when alone

Sarah Bernhardt, *The Star,* *July* 14, 1888
Miss Ward

than before my audience—then I must make them feel—control myself to control them. I have not found that it made any difference with my audience whether I actually shed tears or not—very few *see* the real tear—they *feel* the pathos of the situation, and do good part of the acting themselves.' Miss Mary Anderson's experience tallies curiously with this. While quite a young girl, and before she had any intention of going on the stage, Miss Anderson made the acquaintance of a lady of morbidly lachrymose temperament, who induced in her a horror of this Mrs. Gummidge-like weakness. She therefore deliberately schooled herself in the repression of tears, without any thought of their good or evil effect in acting. The consequence is that neither on nor off the stage do her tears flow very copiously; but they none the less rise to her eyes and make themselves felt in her voice. I have myself seen Miss Anderson's eyes very distinctly suffused at the point in *The Winter's Tale* where Perdita bids Florizel farewell :—

> This dream of mine
> Being now awake, I'll queen it no inch further,
> But milk my ewes and weep ;

and I may add that the thrill of voice with which she spoke these lines (on this particular occasion, at any rate) seemed to me singularly just. Miss Anderson, however, like Miss Ward, feels a part more acutely when not in presence of the audience. ' In my own room at night,' she says, ' when all the house is quiet, I weep and laugh with the character I happen to be studying.' M. Coquelin related to me an anecdote of

Miss Anderson

Mlle. Mars, to the effect that she was one day found *Mlle. Mars*
by a friend bathed in tears, and being asked the
reason, answered, 'Je juge de mes larmes.' We find
Rachel, too, writing to her instructor, Samson, 'J'ai *Rachel.*
étudié mes sanglots (dans le quatrième acte de *Phè-* *D'Heylli,*
dre), je n'ose pas me vanter pour la seconde repré- *p. 26*
sentation, mais je suis sûre qu'ils me viennent.' Miss
Anderson will scarcely admit that in her midnight
vigils with Juliet or Hermione she is testing her tears
and selecting her sobs. Miss Alma Murray tells me *Miss Alma*
that in reading aloud at home or before a private *Murray*
audience she is very apt to break down under stress
of emotion, but that on the stage, though tears come
to her eyes and her voice breaks, she has never felt
any danger of losing her self-control. Thus Miss
Ward, Miss Anderson, and Miss Murray agree in
holding that the mere sight of the footlights tends
to beget that 'temperance' on which Hamlet insists.
Miss Janet Achurch expresses herself very much to *Miss*
the same effect. 'I have often cried bitterly while re- *Achurch*
hearsing a part,' she writes, 'and yet been dry-eyed on
the first performance. Over-nervousness, I suppose,
as in playing the part afterwards the tears have come
back.'

Here let me cite the testimony of Miss Clara *Miss Clara*
Morris, an American actress who is declared by *Morris*
excellent judges to possess, along with some unfortunate mannerisms, a rare and individual genius of
the emotional order. Miss Morris has never appeared
in England, but several English critics who have seen
her have concurred in, and even outdone, the eulogies

The Voice,
x. No. 3
of her countrymen. 'You must feel,' she writes, 'or
all the pretty and pathetic language in the world
won't make other people feel. I never go on the
stage but that about four o'clock in the afternoon I
begin to suffer. My hands get cold as ice, my face
gets hot, and I am in a nervous tremor, because I
am afraid I won't cry in the play. I do everything
to get my feelings thoroughly aroused. Then I only
have to look out for the other danger and keep from
being overcome myself. All the tremolo and false
sobs in the world will never take the place of real
emotion. Of course, after such an emotional effort I
cannot throw the whole effect off, and my poor nerves
suffer.' Miss Morris's theory of art evidently differs
Talma,
*L'Art
Théâtral,
p.* 176
from that of Talma, who, according to Samson, 'se
déclarait mécontent d'un succès qui lui avait coûté
trop de fatigue.' It appears that Miss Morris has
permanently endangered her health by acting at too
high pressure, and this, no doubt, shows either a
morbid temperament or deficient technical training.
At the same time the thrilling effects she produces
are beyond question, however extravagant the price
she pays for them.
Mr. Wilson
Barrett
'Yes,' writes Mr. Wilson Barrett, 'tears come to
my eyes unbidden when I am acting at my best.
With an effort I can repress them, but if I am not
sufficiently in my part for them to come uncalled, no
power of mine can bring them. If one night I have
to simulate what I felt the night before, I should
certainly expect the effect to be lessened. . . . But
mere feeling unguided by art is seldom, if ever,

effective. Art without feeling is better than that, but feeling with art is better than both. The most sensitive organisation, coupled with the highest art, makes the greatest actor. In America you will hear the remark, " Yes, he's a fine artist, but he has no magnetism." In London you will hear people say, " Yes, he's a capital actor, but somehow he never touches me." The meaning is the same ; the fine artist is watched and admired, and often he will get the most praise. He has not stirred the emotions of his audience, and they have had ample time to watch his art. But the actor who feels deeply and guides his emotions by his art will draw to see him hundreds to the other's units.'

'Whether tears do or do not readily come to the eyes,' writes Mr. Beerbohm Tree, 'will depend upon the mere physical development of the individual. Some people have sensitive lachrymal glands, which may be affected by the simple test of the onion— apply the vegetable and the tears will flow. Others, again, have not this physical sensitiveness. It is, therefore, only possible to speak from personal experience. Tears do undoubtedly rise to my eyes in moving situations, perhaps less readily on the stage than in private contemplation. I do not believe that any emotion can be satisfactorily portrayed outside unless the inside emotion exists also ; and I think that the effect upon an audience will generally be in proportion to the power of self-excitation possessed by the actor—given, of course, equal advantages in the way of physique, voice, &c.' Mr. Tree then goes

Mr. Beer-
bohm Tree

on to remark that the use of acquired knowledge, technique, training, canons of art, and so forth, is simply to enable the imagination to work without let or hindrance—to adjust and oil the machinery through which it must give itself utterance.

Mr. John Clayton

Mr. John Clayton,[1] whose Hugh Trevor in *All for Her* is remembered as one of the most pathetic creations of our time, assures me that if tears do not rise spontaneously to his eyes the effect of his acting is distinctly diminished. There are passages in *All for Her* which he has never been able to play without profound emotion—lines which he can scarcely quote in ordinary talk without a tremor in his voice ; and in these passages (as many playgoers well remember) he used to produce upon his audience that highest emotional effect which is expressed, not in immediate applause, but in absorbed, breathless, tearful silence.

Mr. Vezin

Mr. Hermann Vezin is equally decided in his opinion. Tears come readily to his eyes in pathetic situations, and when they fail to come he is conscious of a diminished hold upon his audience. He adds that

C. Kean

Charles Kean, with whom he was long and intimately connected, used to paraphrase Churchill's couplet, and say, ' You must feel yourself, or you'll never make

[1] Mr. Clayton was the first actor (with one exception) who responded to my request for aid in this investigation, and my talk with him in his dressing-room at Toole's Theatre (where he was then playing) was one of the pleasantest and most instructive of many pleasant and instructive interviews. When the above lines first appeared he was yet among us, and we had every reason to hope that the best part of his career, as a manager if not as an actor, lay before him. I cannot place him among actors of the past. He will live for many a day to come in the kindly recollection of thousands.

your audience feel.' Mr. Vezin remarks, however, that the natural breaking of the voice sometimes occurs apart from tears. He mentions an actress of great pathetic power who can produce the most moving tones with perfectly dry eyes; but this he regards as an exception to the rule.

' I have often shed tears in sympathetic situations,' writes Mr. Henry Howe, an excellent actor, and one of the last survivors of a great school, 'especially when aided by the sensibility of the artist who is acting with me. For instance, in the last scene of *Charles I.*, when Huntley leads the children to their mother, I invariably shed tears at the point where Miss Terry, also with tears in her eyes, asks Huntley if the children know of their father's fate. Again, when the King takes leave of Huntley, previous to going to execution, Mr. Irving copiously sheds tears. . . . I have often been told by those who have witnessed the scene that there was scarcely a dry eye in the house.' No one who was near the stage on the first night of *The Amber Heart* can doubt the reality of Miss Ellen Terry's tears. In the second act they literally streamed down her cheeks, while her whole frame was shaken with weeping. Her emotion was not, of course, uncontrollable, but for the moment it was uncontrolled; and I may add that the effect upon the audience was instant and intense.

' In moving situations,' writes Miss Bateman (Mrs. Crowe), ' if real tears do not come to my eyes I do not truly feel what I am acting, nor can I impress my audience to the same extent when I feign

Margin notes:
Mr. Henr Howe

Mr. Irving

Miss Ellen Terry

Miss Bateman

F

emotion as when I really feel it. I have acted the part of Leah for twenty-four years, and the tears always come to my eyes when the little child says "My name is Leah."' Miss Isabel Bateman expresses herself to the same effect.

Mr. Lionel Brough

Mr. Lionel Brough, who, though best known as a comic actor, has every claim to be heard on the question of pathos, writes as follows: 'In moving situations I always cry. I can't help it. My voice goes of its own accord. In a certain pathetic scene of a melodrama, which I played in Liverpool with Miss Phillis Hill, we used every night to agree "not to make fools of ourselves," as we called it; and every night there would be mutual recriminations at the end of the scene, as, "I thought you promised me you wouldn't cry?" Answer, in the same tearful voice (with all the make-up washed off): "So did you, stupid." But neither of us ever regretted the tears, or the way in which the scene went with the audience. If ever I play a pathetic scene with a child (and in most cases with a woman) I am sure to cry. With men, not so; as in any domestic trouble of my own I should endeavour to restrain my tears in telling my sorrows to a man, but should give them free vent in the presence of the other sex. I don't think an actor *ever* can be said to play pathos properly unless he feels it.' Those who have seen Mr. Brough's admirable performance of the old cab-owner in *Retiring* will realise the value of his observations.

Mr. Forbes Robertson

Several of my informants are undecided in their evidence, and of these I may take Mr. Forbes

Robertson as a typical example. 'Tears come to my eyes,' he writes, 'but not unbidden. Neither would I let my voice break of its own accord. I feel all emotional scenes, under favourable conditions, very strongly, but I never dare let myself go. Nevertheless I like to persuade myself that I am, for the time being, the person I am playing ; to surrender myself to the passion of the moment, and only to know myself, as it were, sufficiently to prevent breaking down. . . . Phelps often shed tears. On one occasion when I was playing with him in an emotional scene, being young and much affected at his acting and my own emotions, I got beyond my own control. Phelps afterwards warned me, and admitted that he might easily be carried away by an affecting scene did he not keep a strict watch on himself.' On the whole, I think, Mr. Forbes Robertson may be said to take the emotional side, though he dwells more than some of his comrades on the necessity for keeping a tight rein on the feelings. One of the few decided disbelievers in emotion is Mr. Frank Harvey, who writes as follows : 'The late Mademoiselle Beatrice, with whom I was long associated, moved her audience to tears to a painful degree ; but she felt little emotion herself. On the other hand, when acting with the late Miss Neilson, I have seen real tears streaming down her cheeks, but I don't think she moved her audience any more.' Miss Neilson's extreme susceptibility to emotion seems to have been quite incommensurate with her power of producing pathetic effect. But then no one supposes

[margin: Phelps]

[margin: Mlle. Beatrice]

[margin: Miss Neilson]

F 2

that an actress's command over her audience is proportionate to the mere quantity of her tears.

The most resolute upholder of the non-emotional theory with whom I have come in contact is Mr. A. W. Pinero, whose keen intelligence and wide knowledge of the stage, both as actor and author, must give his opinions exceptional weight. He does not deny that tears are shed, but he argues that they are not a true sign of feeling, and that actors deceive themselves in supposing that they are. With a week's practice, he says, anyone can learn to produce tears at will. You have only to 'breathe, not through the nose, but through the closed throat'—that is, as I understand it, to produce mechanically the *globus hystericus*. That thoughtful young actor Mr. Bernard Gould makes a similar assertion. ' I have frequently,' he writes, ' found it possible at a moment's notice, and without any (even simulated) affecting surroundings, to force tears into the eyes by merely speaking in a mechanically-produced broken voice.' This is a curious testimony to the intimate connection between the muscles of the throat and lachrymal glands. Mr. Pinero proceeds to maintain that in many actors the habit of thus ' pumping up' tears becomes a second nature, and almost a disease. He mentions a well-known actress who could read you a comic poem, weeping copiously all the time ; and a popular actor who, even in private life, could scarcely relate an ordinary incident, such as having seen a horse fall in the street, without being bathed in tears. Miss Wallis, who studied acting under the late John Ryder, gives me a curious case

Mr. Pinero

Mr. B. Gould

John Ryder

in point. She once expressed to her instructor her wonder at the way in which an actress much in vogue at the time managed to turn on tears wherever there was the slightest excuse for them. ' Look at me, my dear,' Mr. Ryder replied ; and instantly she saw a tear gather in his eye and roll slowly down his cheek !

Another strong argument of Mr. Pinero's is that, in a part with which he is quite familiar, an actor will often produce a powerful effect upon his audience in total unconsciousness of what he is doing ; just as some people will read aloud whole pages of a book, intelligently enough to all appearance, and will suddenly wake up to the fact that their thoughts have been absent, and that they do not know a single word they have been reading. Of this Miss Mary Anderson relates a curious instance. After the fourth act of *Romeo and Juliet*, one night, her maid began to unfasten her dress in order to put on the white draperies of the Tomb scene. 'Don't do that,' said Miss Anderson ; ' I have to play the Potion scene yet '; and it took some time to convince her that she had not only just played it, but had played (as her comrades assured her, and as the applause of the audience showed) with unusual effect. I could adduce several similar cases. It is said that Mr. and Mrs. Alfred Wigan, having made some mistake in a cue at the end of an important scene, actually played the whole scene over again in blissful unconsciousness of their blunder. John Ireland relates how poor Reddish, when his faculties were failing, played Posthumus for his benefit under the full conviction that he was playing

[Miss Anderson]

[Mr. and Mrs. Wigan]

[Reddish Ireland, p. 58]

Romeo! 'I congratulated him on his being enough recovered to perform. Yes, sir, replied he, I shall perform, and in the garden scene I shall astonish you! —In the garden scene, Mr. Reddish?—I thought you were to play Posthumus—No, sir, I play Romeo. . . At the time appointed he set out for the Theatre. The gentleman who went with him . . . told me that his mind was so imprest with the character of Romeo, he was reciting it all the way. . . . When the time came for his appearance, they pushed him on the stage, fearing he would begin with a speech of Romeo. With the same expectation I stood in the pit. . . . The instant he came in sight of the audience his recollection seemed to return . . . he made the bow of modest respect, and went through the scene much better than I had ever before seen him. On his return to the green-room the image of Romeo returned to his mind.' We have here a real 'paradox of acting'; but I doubt whether such freaks of consciousness can be made to tell either for or against Diderot's argument.

Mr. Toole

'No audience, in my opinion,' says Mr. Toole, ' was ever made to weep unless the actor had wept, or could weep, at what touched the audience. At the same time, an actor must be able to control himself.' That is the real turning-point of the whole discussion. The anti-emotionalists from Diderot, or rather from François Riccoboni, onwards, assume that real emotion is inconsistent with self-control ; whereas the emotionalists argue (as I think, justly) that the accomplished actor is he who, in the moment of performance, can freely utilise the subtle action of the imagination upon the organs of expression, without running the least risk of its overmastering him. The illustration given by Mr. Lawrence Barrett in a recent 'interview' is very much to the point. Mr. Barrett says : 'In my opinion the prime requisites of an actor are sensibility and imagination. But he must have these under perfect control. The moment that they become his masters instead of his servants, he ceases to be an artist. Mr. Booth and I were discussing this point the other day, and he gave this illustration. A friend invites you out to take a drive behind two high-spirited horses, that can go in, say 2.30. He speeds them along at, perhaps, a three-minute gait, and you admire his control of them. Presently the horses get fuller of spirit, their enthusiasm is communicated to the driver. He lets them out, nay, he even urges them on to their fastest pace, but he doesn't lose control over them. If he did they would soon be running away with him. You see the delight in his face, the eagerness to get the best out of his animals, you appreciate and enjoy his excitement, which is communicated to you, but you have confidence that he remains master. So it is with acting. The actor's powers and feelings will sometimes carry him along faster than at others, but he must always keep a strong hand over them.' To the same effect writes Miss Clara Morris. 'As to really losing oneself in a part, that will not do : it is worse to be too sympathetic than to have too much art. I must cry in my

Mr. Lawrence Barrett, New York Tribune, December 18, 1887

Mr. Edwin Booth

Miss Clara Morris, Matthews and Hutton, v. p. 224

emotional *rôles* and feel enough to cry, but I must not allow myself to become so affected as to mumble my words, to redden my nose, or to become hysterical.'

Some actors (a very small percentage) do undoubtedly suffer from their inability to keep their feelings properly in check. Of Walker, a tragedian of some note, though chiefly remembered as the original Macheath in the *Beggar's Opera*, the author of *The Actor* writes :—' His ruin was that his sensibility continually ran away with him ; . . . the blood was in his face before the time, his whole person was disordered, and unless people knew the part, they could not find out for what ; for the vehemence of his feeling took away his utterance. *Vox faucibus hæsit*, and he could not speak articulately.' The same writer tells of a Mr. Berry, whose excessive sensibility injured his playing in all parts save that of Adam, in *As You Like It*, where it stood him in good stead. ' I remember a great tragedian, Powell,' says Cape Everard, ' performing the part of Jaffier, and when he said,

I have not wrong'd thee—by these tears I have not,

his feelings were so great that they choaked his utterance, his articulation was lost, his face was drowned in tears.—The audience from these causes, not understanding what he said, the effect was of course lost. When Garrick, in the same part, spoke the same line, every eye in the house dropt a tear ! If he did not feel himself he made everybody else feel.'

Servandoni d'Hannetaire, again, who published a book of *Observations sur l'Art du Comédien* in 1776,

Marginal notes:
Walker

Ed. 1755, *p.* 82

Powell, *Everard*, *p.* 5

Hannetaire

quotes the younger Riccoboni's remarks on the danger *Ante, p.* 15
of tears, and then adds, 'Bien des Acteurs, comme
nous, ont été obligés d'abandonner le genre pathétique
par rapport à cette pente excessive à l'attendrissement
et au trop de facilité à répandre des larmes.' Since
M. d'Hannetaire avers that this was his own case, we
have no reason to doubt him ; but it is certainly rarer
than he seems to suppose. The exaggeration which
we call 'ranting' is, indeed, common enough, but that
is due, not to excess of uncontrolled sensibility, but to
imperfect technical training and defective taste. Many
artists, as we have seen, concur in holding that the
mere presence of the audience is sufficient to beget the
necessary self-command, and M. d'Hannetaire is the
only player I ever heard of who was forced by a too
copious flux of tears either to abandon the stage or to
confine himself to comic characters.

It is obvious that even a consummate artist may,
on occasion, be carried beyond himself to the detriment of the desired effect. An anecdote of Molé, *viii. p.* 346
quoted in Assézat's notes to the *Paradoxe*, affords a
case in point. Lemercier was so much charmed with Molé
Molé's acting one evening that he rushed to congra-
tulate him. Molé replied that he was not pleased
with his own performance, and had not affected the
audience as much as usual. ' Je me suis trop livré,'
he said, 'je n'étais plus maître de moi ; j'étais entré
si vivement dans la situation que j'étais le personnage même, et que je n'étais plus l'acteur qui le joue ;
j'ai été vrai comme je le serais chez moi, mais pour
l'optique du théâtre, il faut l'être autrement.' He

begged Lemercier to come and see him again when the piece was repeated. Lemercier did so, taking his station at the wing, and as Molé passed him to go òn the stage he whispered, ' Je suis bien maître de moi, vous allez voir.' Lemercier declares that, as Molé predicted, he produced a much greater effect on the second occasion than on the first. The brothers Mounet, the leading tragedians of the contemporary French stage, both convinced champions of the emotional theory, are subject to occasional failures of self-control.

M. Paul
Mounet,
*Revue
d'Art
Drama-
tique, v.
p. 291*

Paul Mounet, of the Odéon, admits that he now and then yields to a delicious ' intoxication ' of feeling ; but returning sobriety brings with it self-criticism and dissatisfaction. The aforesaid Molé summed up in a single phrase the true artistic principle. ' Au théâtre,' he used to say, ' il faut livrer son cœur et garder sa tête.'

M. Lam-
bert

M. Albert Lambert père, a highly esteemed actor of the Odéon, expresses himself in almost identical terms. ' Comme principe général sur mon art,' he writes, ' j'ai celui-ci : *Le cœur chaud, la tête froide.* J'entends par *cœur* : les facultés cérébrales, qui peuvent conserver la sensibilité à l'état ardent, qui savent appeler les larmes par un simple effort de volonté : les suffocations, les angoisses, toutes les affres de la douleur, soit en souvenir des situations semblables vues ou éprouvées dans la vie, soit par l'identification voulue avec le personnage qu'on représente. Par *tête froide* : le pouvoir directeur toujours en éveil, une espèce d'instinct de conservation artistique qui, dans la plus affolée des explosions, sait la diriger selon les lois d'un art appris et médité.'

Finally, let me quote from J. J. Engel's *Ideen zu einer* | Berlin.
Mimik, the views of a very penetrating critic of last | 1785-86
century, who, though not an actor himself, was for
some years a manager, and lived in hourly communion
with actors. ' Actors,' he says, 'all speak of *feeling*, | Engel
and think that they are certain to play excellently
if . . . they fill themselves with the enthusiasm of
their subject. I can cite only one (but he certainly
the greatest) actor I have known, our *Eckhof* to wit, | Eckhof
who, neither in regard to declamation nor to action,
relied on feeling alone ; but rather in the moment of
performance kept himself in hand so as not to fall
into an excess of feeling, and, from lack of self-
command, play with defective truth, expression, harmony, and finish. . . . I know actors who can in a
single moment fill their eyes with tears. . . . Happy
he who possesses this gift, and knows how to govern
it wisely ; for a falling tear is often, unquestionably,
of excellent effect ; but to heat the fancy to such
a degree that its suggestions become as moving as
reality itself, seems to me a dangerous course. . . .
Real emotions too easily take possession of the whole
heart and obstruct or distort the utterance they are
designed to intensify.' If this tendency be so potent
in any particular case that it must at all costs be
eradicated, then, doubtless, the player should school
himself to automatism. But to make automatism an
imperative ideal for all is like condemning the whole
world to total abstinence because one man in ten
thousand is a dipsomaniac.

CHAPTER V.

'ET MENTEM MORTALIA TANGUNT.'

'TEARS,' say the upholders of Diderot, 'are no trustworthy sign of feeling. An onion or a grain of sand
will call them up just as readily as the agony of Alkestis
or the woes of Ophelia. The practised actor can produce them mechanically if he thinks it worth while,
and with some the habit of producing them for any

Pollock,
p. 16

reason, or no reason, becomes a disease. The Master
himself permits his ideal actor to weep, so long as he
has arranged beforehand "the precise moment at which
to produce his handkerchief, the word, the syllable at
which his tears must flow."' Are there no cases, then
in which we can prove that the actor is really feeling
in his own person something similar in kind, if not
equal in degree, to the emotion he is representing? It
was the object of my second question to elicit evidence
on this point. The original wording (as the reader
may see by turning to the Appendix) was not quite
accurate. This is how I should have put the point :—

When Macready played Virginius shortly after the death
of a favourite daughter, the thought of her, as he confessed,
mingled with, and intensified, his mourning for Virginia. Have
you any analogous experience to relate? Has a personal

emotion (whether recent or remote) influenced your acting in a situation which tended to revive it? If so, was the influence, in your opinion, for good or ill? And what was the effect upon the audience?

Personal emotion may influence acting in two ways. The actor may consciously or unconsciously note the external manifestations of his feeling while it is actually upon him (Talma and Rachel are said to have noted them consciously), and then 'may voluntarily reproduce or mimic them on the stage without again experiencing the slightest emotion, just as he might mimic the gesture or accent of some totally indifferent person. This process, as a writer in the *Westminster Review* has remarked, 'substantially squares with Wordsworth's canon of poetic composition—that it is emotion recollected in tranquillity.' The next question bears upon this point, not the question now before us. What I here wanted to get at was the direct influence of real and present personal emotion upon acting. I wanted to learn how far, and with what effect, personal sorrow tends to mingle with the imaginary woes of the theatre. If we find that actors who profess to 'feel' recognise no essential distinction, but at most a mere difference of degree between purely mimetic emotion and personal sorrow revived by the similarity of their mimic to their real situation, then, surely, we shall be justified in concluding that mimetic emotion and personal emotion belong to the same order of mental phenomena, however much they may differ in poignancy and persistency.

The classical case in point is that of the Greek

Post, pp. 98, 99

N. S. vol. lxxi. p. 55

Polus,

Demo-
sthenes,
xxviii.

Noctes
Atticæ,
vii. 5

actor Polus, declared by Plutarch to have been un-
equalled in his craft. Aulus Gellius is our authority
for the anecdote. 'Polus, therefore,' he says, 'clad in
the mourning habit of Electra, took from the tomb
the bones and urn of his son, and as if embracing
Orestes, filled the place, not with the image and imitation, but with the sighs and lamentations of unfeigned
sorrow. Therefore, when a fable seemed to be represented, real grief was displayed.' This anecdote is
often loosely cited with the addition that the actor's
unwonted fervour produced an unwonted effect upon.

Pollock,
p. 107

the audience. Even Diderot seems to have fallen
into this error. Aulus Gellius says nothing whatever about the effect on the audience. The anecdote shows that a protagonist whom the Athenians
reckoned great believed in the good effect of real
emotion on the stage, and did not shrink from an
extravagant device for securing the genuine article.
It proves 'only this and nothing more.'

ii. p. 159

In Barry Cornwall's *Life of Edmund Kean* we
find a strange instance of the deliberate and calculated
infusion of personal feeling into a theatrical situation.

Edmund
Kean

One of the great little man's most striking successes
was achieved in Maturin's tragedy of *Bertram*. 'The
benediction " God bless the child," ' says his biographer,
' for which Kean obtained so much applause, had been
previously uttered a hundred times over his own son
Charles. He repeated it so often, and so fervently,
that he became touched by the modulation of his own
voice ; which, under the before-mentioned circumstances, acquired a tenderness " beyond the reach of

art."' This elaborate working-up and dragging-in of paternal feeling tallies, in a sense, with both emotionalist and anti-emotionalist theory. Diderot would greatly have approved of the hundredfold rehearsal, but would have held the utilisation of 'Charles his son' an unworthy lapse into sensibility. The truly great actor, according to his theory, would have lavished his blessings just as fervently on a chair or a coal-box. And here, I grant, Diderot might have claimed the authority of Garrick, if we may believe one of Cape Everard's anecdotes. Everard, then a boy, was playing Thomas, Duke of Clarence, in the second part of *King Henry IV*. After the first rehearsal, Garrick called him 'into the Great Green Room ; Mrs. Pritchard, Mrs. Yates, and many others, the first performers there. He told me that I spoke the part extremely well, only one line he wished me to give with a little more feeling. -I said, "Oh yes, sir, I intend to do so at night." He caught at my expression as if lightning had shot athwart him !— "At night !" says he, "why, can you speak or play better at *night* than in the *morning*? . . . Then, sir, you are no actor ! I suppose, too, you could give Romeo's, or Jaffier's speech, of

> Oh woman, woman, lovely, charming woman !

with more softness and feeling if you addressed it to Mrs. Yates there, than you could to this marble slab?"' The boy owned the soft impeachment ; whereupon Garrick continued, 'Then, you are no actor ! If you cannot give a speech, or make love to a table, chair,

Garrick,
Everard,
p. 4

or marble, as well as to the finest woman in the world, you are not, nor ever will be a great actor ! '

Macready

Macready's daughter Nina died on February 24, 1850. On November 14 he notes: ' Acted Virginius. . . . I kept my mind on the part, and acted it, certainly, never better. The audience was extraordinarily excited. . . . In the second act my thoughts so fixed upon my blessed Nina that my emotion nearly overpowered me.' Again, on January 3, 1851,

Reminiscences, ii. *pp.* 358, 363

he writes : ' Acted Virginius, one of the most brilliant and powerful performances of the character I have ever given. I did indeed " gore my own thoughts " to do it, for my own Katie was in my mind, as in one part the tears streamed down my cheeks ; and, in another, she who is among the blest, beloved one ! Such is a player's mind and heart ! Called.' In these cases there can surely be no doubt that Macready did feel. The mimic situation reopened a real and recent wound, and the personal sorrow reinforced the mimic emotion, both together acting potently upon his physical organism. Nor can there be any doubt that he believed the effect upon his acting to be for good, and that the enthusiasm of the audience gave him valid ground for this belief. Note that, on the first occasion, his emotion ' nearly overpowered him.' Nearly, but not quite, for he was a consummate artist ; and so long as it did not quite carry him away he had nothing to reproach himself with. On the contrary, ' the audience was extraordinarily excited.'

Lady Martin

Miss Helen Faucit (Lady Martin) relates a similar event in her own experience. A few days after learning of the death of her dearly-loved sister, she had to appear at a benefit (sorely against her will) in some scenes from *Romeo and Juliet*. It was represented to her that the charity would suffer by her failure to perform, and she resolved to make the effort. ' I got on very well,' she writes, ' in the scene with the Friar. There was despair in it, but nothing that in any way touched upon my own trial. My great struggle was in Juliet's chamber when left alone. Then her desolation, her loneliness, became mine, and the rushing tears would have way. Happily the fearful images presented to Juliet's mind of what is before her in the tomb soon sent softer feelings away; but how glad I was when the fancied sight of Tybalt's ghost allowed the grief that was in my heart to find vent in a wild cry of anguish as well as horror !' This passage is particularly interesting because it lays stress on the analogy between the real and the mimic situation, showing how the sorrow in Miss Faucit's heart at once rushed into the channel provided for it by Juliet's lonely anguish.

Shake-speare's Female Characters, p. 130

Perhaps the most touching instance on record of the mingling of personal with mimetic emotion is to be found in Legouvé's account of a midnight rehearsal of *Adrienne Lecouvreur*, very shortly before its production. Legouvé himself, Régnier, Maillard, and Rachel had remained behind all the rest, when Rachel proposed that they should go over the fifth act once more. No sooner had she commenced than Legouvé was struck by the intense and unusual pathos in Rachel's voice. She played the whole scene with heartrending

Soixante Ans de Souvenirs, ii. p. 228

G

power, and the three auditors were visibly moved. After it was over Rachel sat silent in a corner of the green-room, still weeping and shaken by nervous tremors. Legouvé went up to her and said : 'Ma chère amie, vous avez joué ce cinquième acte comme vous ne le jouerez jamais de votre vie !' 'Je le crois,' she replied, 'et savez-vous pourquoi ? . . . Ce n'est pas sur Adrienne que j'ai pleuré, c'est sur moi ! Un je ne sais quoi m'a dit tout à coup que je mourrais jeune comme elle ; il m'a semblé que j'étais dans ma propre chambre, à ma dernière heure, que j'assistais à ma propre mort. Aussi lorsqu'à cette phrase "Adieu triomphes du théâtre ! Adieu ivresses d'un art que j'ai tant aimé " vous m'avez vu verser des larmes véritables, c'est que j'ai pensé avec désespoir, que le temps emporterait toute trace de ce qui aura été mon talent, et que bientôt—il ne resterait plus rien de celle qui fut Rachel !' This anecdote reminds one of the extreme emotion displayed by the American actor Thomas A. Cooper (the pupil of William Godwin), in acting Wolsey, at a time when his fame and fortune were on the wane. Tears coursed down his cheeks in the scene with Cromwell, and those who knew him best believed that he was overcome by the analogy between Wolsey's situation and his own.

We are indebted to M. Coquelin, curiously enough, for one of the most interesting of the anecdotes bearing on this point. One morning, in the spring of 1849, he says, Régnier was crossing the Pont des Arts with his little daughter. The child ran away from him ; he chased her, caught her, lifted her up, and kissed

Ludlow, p. 371

Régnier

L'Art et le Comédien, p. 31

her, 'd'un mouvement admirable de paternité heureuse.'
' Bravo ! ' said someone behind them, applauding as if
in the theatre ; and, turning, the comedian recognised
Emile Augier. Borrowing the words of Henri IV.
when found playing with his children, Régnier said :
' Etes-vous père, Monsieur l'Ambassadeur ? ' and they
passed on laughing. Three months afterwards, Augier
stood with Régnier at the little girl's grave. He was
then giving the final touches to his *Gabrielle*, and on
returning from the cemetery he added to Julien's part
in the fifth act, the lines :

> Nous n'existons vraiment que par ces petits êtres
> Qui dans tout notre cœur s'établissent en maîtres,
> Qui prennent notre vie et ne s'en doutent pas,
> Et n'ont qu'à vivre heureux pour n'être point ingrats.

' Et ces vers, si charmants et si vrais, à quelque temps
de là, le père lui-même les disait sur la scène, impo-
sant comme artiste silence à ses douleurs, ou plutôt,
par une espèce de courage propre à notre art, les
pétrissant avec celles de son rôle pour en faire une
création admirable.' It seems to me that in admitting
the good effect of this 'kneading together' of real
with imagined feeling, M. Coquelin practically aban-
dons his anti-emotionalist position.

' Macready's experience,' writes Signor Salvini,   Salvini
' has also been mine. One evening, in *Le Marbrier*
by Alexandre Dumas père, I had to play the part of
a father who has lost his daughter. That very evening, my own daughter, three years old, lay on her
death-bed ! My tears choked my voice, and my sobs
went so directly to the heart of the audience that their

Ristori

enthusiasm was intense.' 'Many and many a time,' writes Salvini's countrywoman and sister-artist Ristori, 'in sustaining the part of a daughter who loses her parents or of a mother who sees her sons in the grasp of death, my tears have blinded me, and I have felt my heart bursting with sorrow. I have occasionally been so overcome by the analogy between a fictitious situation and an event in my own life, that I have had to put forth all my strength in order to retain my self-control, and have not always entirely succeeded! The effects obtained under such mental conditions are naturally stronger because they are truer.' Diderot meets with short shrift at the hands of the great Italians.

Most of my informants, however, who have anything to say on this point, agree that a too recent sorrow is hurtful. Mr. John Clayton went from the deathbed of his father to play in a similar scene, and utterly broke down. In other cases in which a stage situation has recalled a recent personal trouble, the effect upon his acting was bad, as he did not dare to let himself go. It will be remembered that during the historic run of *Hamlet* at the Lyceum in 1874–75, Mr. H. L. Bateman, the manager, died. His daughter, Miss Isabel Bateman, was playing Ophelia to Mr. Irving's Hamlet, and had to resume the part after a very short intermission. 'The effect of the real experience,' Miss Bateman writes, 'was anything but beneficial to my performance. In my effort for self-control I believe I never acted so badly; it remains in my memory as a terrible nightmare, and I have had a horror of the

Mr. Clayton

Miss Isabel Bateman

part ever since.' When we think of such speeches as
' I would give you some violets, but they withered all
when my father died,' we can easily conceive what a
terrible ordeal this must have been. ' On the other
hand,' Miss Bateman continues, ' my acting has been
greatly influenced for good by real but more remote
sorrows.' ' The death of a beloved female relative,'
writes Mr. John Coleman, an actor trained in the
school of Macready, ' affected me so much that while
playing Hamlet, soon afterwards, I was carried quite
beyond myself in the scene of Ophelia's funeral, and
overcome by an attack of semi-hysterical emotion.
Although I have no personal knowledge or recollection of the effect upon the audience, I was assured
that both actors and audience were very much
excited by the occurrence.' It is curious that Mr.
Coleman and Macready should use the same word,
' excited,' to indicate the effect upon an audience of
a performance in which personal sorrow intensified
the mimic emotion of the scene. The difference
between the two cases is that, whereas Macready
himself observes and reports the excitement of the
audience, Mr. Coleman confesses that he was too
much carried away to observe anything. I take it
that Mr. Coleman does not consider the ' excitement '
he created an artistically desirable effect. It is certain
that where a player (in Macready's phrase) is too
obviously ' goring his own thoughts,' the effect cannot
but be crudely painful, like that of a bull-fight or of
a gladiatorial display. Yet the fact that powerful

*Mr. John
Coleman*

effects, however undesirable, have been and can be produced under these circumstances, is a sufficient disproof of Diderot's argument that real emotion on the stage is of necessity 'paltry and weak,' meagre and unconvincing.

Two very distinguished actresses have been good enough to communicate to me experiences which exactly illustrate the influence upon acting of recent and of more remote personal sorrow. Even in her early girlhood—from the age of sixteen onwards— Miss Madge Robertson used to play the part of Lady Isabel Carlyle (afterwards Madame Vigne) in a dramatic version of *East Lynne.* She used to mourn over the dying child without knowing what sorrow meant. Then she became Mrs. Kendal ; and, in the loss of her first child, she learned to sympathise only too vividly with the distracted mother of the play. *East Lynne* was at this time vastly popular, especially with Saturday-night audiences ; and on a Saturday evening, less than a fortnight after her bereavement, Mrs. Kendal had to play Lady Isabel before a crowded audience at Hull. Everything, even to the name of the child, reminded her of her loss ; and in the third act her emotion became so heartrending that she was utterly overpowered by it, and the curtain had to be dropped before the end of the act. The effect upon the audience was electrical and thrilling. A woman stood up in the pit and cried, ' No more ! no more ! ' But it was not an effect which, either as a woman or an artist, Mrs. Kendal could bring herself to repeat. She got through the last act as best she might, and

Mrs.
Kendal

from that day to this has never reappeared in *East Lynne*.[1]

This was an instance in which acute and present personal sorrow absorbed rather than reinforced the mimic emotion, and changed the imagined heroine's imagined agony into real torture for the real woman. We come now to a case in which the memory of a more remote sorrow has aided in the production of an effect, the pathos of which must be fresh in the minds of thousands of playgoers. Mrs. Bancroft writes as follows : ' When a circumstance on the stage strikes home, reminding me of a great grief, a domestic sorrow, or a grievous wrong, it must for the time being cause a feeling of pain which of necessity gives an impetus to my acting. I can well sympathise with Macready, and understand how the loss of a loved child would affect his acting in *Virginius*. . . . When I played the Vicar's wife in *The Vicarage*, I had to deliver a particular speech which always affected me deeply : " God gave me a little child ; but then, when all was bright and beautiful, God took His gift away," &c. The remembrance of the death of my own child was revived in these words. My heart was full of his image, and my tears came in tribute to his memory. I could not have stopped them if I had tried.' No one, surely, will maintain that Mrs. Bancroft deceives

Mrs. Bancroft

[1] As an instance of that mingling of the grotesque with the tragic which makes such a motley web of life, I may mention that Mrs. Kendal remembers vividly the broad Yorkshire accent of the child who played little Willie. His last words were : ' A cannut see yu or eear yur voïce. A can oanly eear the singin' of those voïces in the shinin' gärden. Theear ! Theear ! '

herself in supposing that she was feeling with her character—that is to say, was going through in her own
·person something very like the mental experience
(with its physical accompaniments) attributed by the
author to Mrs. Haygarth. 'The effect upon my audience,' Mrs. Bancroft continues—and no one who saw
The Vicarage need be reminded of this—' was that
not a heart amongst them did not feel with me. Their
silence spoke volumes, and their tears told me of their
sympathy.'

Miss Ward

Miss Geneviève Ward, though doubtful as to the
artistic effect of personal emotion, has no doubt as to
its tendency to mingle with the emotion of the scene.
' Many sad experiences in my life,' she writes, ' have
helped to intensify my feelings on the stage, even
though not strictly analogous ; but I have not found
that it made any difference in the effect upon my
audience. The influence on myself was to make me
suffer, not only from the sorrow, but from the effort to
control my feelings and keep them within the bounds
of the situation. I have seen a young actress, whose
pathos rarely touched her audience, perform one night
under the influence of the deepest sorrow, tears rolling
down her cheeks freely, and sobs breaking her voice.
Yet the audience was quite as unmoved as on other
occasions in the same situation.' This proves, what
is sufficiently obvious, that emotion alone, without the
faculty of dramatic expression, will not make itself
felt across the footlights; and the proof of this fact is
mistaken by some supporters of Diderot for the proof

Mr. Wilson
Barrett

of his theory. Mr. Wilson Barrett mentions several

analogous cases to the one just quoted. 'I have seen an emotional novice,' he writes, 'drown herself in tears. Evidently she has been torn with emotion, but, beyond the tears, there has been absolutely no outward and visible sign of this inward and spiritual suffering. I have again and again held a mirror to a young actor, and when he has evidently been feeling deeply, his face, to his astonishment, has borne a peaceful, placid smile.' All this merely shows that the use of inward emotion is to reinforce, not to supplant, outward expression. No one has ever doubted that the actor must be able to express what he feels, or feeling will avail him nothing. The question at issue is whether he ought, or ought not, to feel what he expresses.

Returning to the special subject of personal emotion, I am glad to be able to cite the experience of two actors who (as I can vouch from my own observation) have been most successful in mastering and moving the vast audiences of East End and suburban theatres. In the West End Mr. George Conquest is chiefly known as a pantomimist, but he is also a melodramatic actor of rare intensity. He, like Macready, has had to appear in a situation reminding him of the loss of a beloved daughter; and he, too, felt his personal sorrow mingle with his mimic emotion. 'I think,' he writes, 'the influence may have been good while the situation applied, but afterwards it distracted the mind from the true object of the drama.' Mr. J. H. Clynds, again, gives me his experience as follows :—'I was one night playing Hamlet during a short starring engagement, while my father lay dead

Mr. Conquest

Mr. Clynds

at home ; and during the whole of the first act the tears
were literally streaming down my face. At the line
" My father !—methinks I see my father ! " it was only
with the greatest effort that I could proceed. . . . The
audience knew nothing of the (to me) sad event, and
what effect was created I was too much engrossed to
observe ; but it was afterwards conveyed to me that
it was a matter of general comment that night, " What
wonderful pathos the Hamlet possessed, and what a
voice of tears ! " ' In answer to my first question Mr.
Clynds writes, ' It has always made itself felt to me
that I produce a greater effect with *real* tears and the
genuine lump in the throat than when these affections
are not physically experienced '; and Mr. Clynds, I
repeat, is an actor to whose strong hold upon large
popular audiences I can myself bear witness. Now,
if real feeling on the stage were, as many anti-emotionalists contend, absolutely and essentially ineffec-
tive, it certainly would not tell at the Grecian and the
Adelphi any more than at the Lyceum. I would
therefore lay stress on the testimony of Mr. Conquest
and Mr. Clynds as showing that, whatever its artistic
value, real sorrow does mingle with mimic emotion,
and (to state the case in the most guarded terms) at
least does not annul the desired effect.

The remaining answers to this question must be
briefly summarised. Among the artists who assure
me that personal sorrows have influenced their acting, and, as they believe, for good, I may mention M.
Albert Lambert père, Mr. Wilson Barrett, Mr. Forbes
Robertson, Miss Wallis, Miss Maud Milton, Miss

Dorothy Dene, Mr. Leonard Boyne, and Mr. Leonard
Outram. Mr. Outram writes, 'The public has frequently been agreeably surprised by the sudden ac-
cession of pathetic power in an actor or actress who
has for the first time in a happy life encountered a
domestic affliction.' Mr. Herbert Standing, again,
sends me the following note :—' I have been playing
Triplet in *Masks and Faces* lately, and in the scene
where he speaks of his starving children I could not
but think of my motherless little ones. I always got
the right feeling and the " lump in the throat," along
with the appreciation of the audience.'

Many of my informants, happily, have no experience of the effect of personal sorrow upon art.
Others say that their domestic griefs are 'too sacred'
to be ' used ' on the stage ; meaning, I presume, that
in a situation recalling any private sorrow, they would
make a deliberate effort to forget or ignore the analogy. This implies a curious mental state or faculty,
of no importance, however, to our present inquiry.

The purport of this section, let me repeat, is
primarily to prove that actual emotion is felt on the
stage, and only in the second place to test its artistic
value. My object has been to rebut the assertion
that what actors describe and think of as 'feeling' is
merely a state of nervous excitement not in the least
resembling the emotional condition they have to por-
tray. I have shown that the actor does, in some cases,
indubitably feel with his character, the imagined emotion happening to coincide with a real emotion in
his real life. It is pretty clear, too, I think, from the

answers I have quoted, that the effect upon the actor
of this mingling of real with imagined emotion differs
in degree rather than in kind from the effect of the
imagined emotion, pure and simple, to which my first
question referred. If so, is there not at least a very
strong probability that the artists who say that they
'feel' are not deceiving themselves, and that, in the
particular order of emotions in question, the imagination can, and does, beget in the actor's mind and body
a condition more or less analogous to that of the
character he represents?

Sorrow is not, of course, the only emotion which
may transfuse itself from the real man or woman into
the imaginary personage, though for the reasons indicated above it is by far the most important. Joy
will be dealt with in a later chapter; in the meantime
let me say a few words as to love, hate, and their
kindred sentiments.

We have seen how Sainte-Albine, followed by his
English adaptor, and by Sticotti, asserted roundly
that 'Les personnes nées pour aimer devroient avoir
seules le privilège de jouer les rôles d'Amans.' An
obvious corollary to this principle is that only an
actor and actress who are positively in love with each
other can do justice to Romeo and Juliet; the author
of *The Actor* even going so far as to assert, with
refreshing cynicism, 'that husband and wife have
seldom been observed to play the lovers well upon
the stage.' Diderot, of course, rebuts the extravagant
assumption that stage lovers must be lovers in reality,

Ante, p. 38

Ed. 1755,
p. 196

Pollock, p.
48

and his remarks on the subject led me, in my first interrogatory, to put a question as to the effect of personal 'likes and dislikes' upon acting.

The general tenor of the answers was precisely what I anticipated. Unlike the simple emotions, love and hatred do not manifest themselves in characteristic and unmistakable external symptoms. They are emotional attitudes rather than individual emotions. Personal feelings of this sort, then, can but little help or hinder dramatic expression, any influence they may possibly possess being quite indirect. Dramatic annals, it is true, abound in anecdotes of lovers throwing exceptional fervour into love-scenes, and even of haters giving treble force to passages of invective. In most of these cases, however, there is probably a lurking fallacy of observation. Spectators who know, believe, or suspect that a certain personal relation exists between two artists, are apt to see 'confirmation strong' in trifles light as air, and to make much of differences which are imperceptible to the uninitiated. More than any other members of society (princes, perhaps, excepted), actors and actresses are the favourite playthings of gossip. To see beneath the mask, to discover personal warmth in mimic caresses and personal bitterness in mimic scorn, gives the theatrical busybody a sense of superiority. The wish is so apt to beget the thought that we cannot accept such evidence without suspicion.

One of the most famous instances of lovers excelling in a drama of love is thus quaintly related by the brothers Parfaict:—'Le mercredi premier

Baron jun. and Mlle. Desmares,

Histoire du Théâtre-Français, *xiv. p.* 307

Juin [1703], les comédiens remirent au Théatre la Tragédie-Ballet de Psyché, de M. Moliere, qui eut vingt neuf représentations. . . . Ce qui contribua beaucoup au succès de cette remise, c'est que . . . l'Actrice qui représentoit le personnage de Psyché (Mademoiselle Desmares) et l'Acteur qui jouoit celui de l'Amour (M. Baron, fils) quoiqu' excellens tous deux, se surpasserent encore dans ces deux rôles ; on dit qu'ils ressentoient l'un pour l'autre la plus vive tendresse, et que leurs talens supérieurs ne furent employés que pour marquer avec plus de précision les sentimens de leurs cœurs.' It is said that the

Lema-zurier, *i. p.* 120

fervour of Psyche's passion for Cupid was so obvious as to lead to explanations between the actress and her 'amant en titre,' the Duc d'Orléans, which resulted in her giving the prince his dismissal and installing

Gueullette, *p.* 20

the actor in his stead. A less pleasant anecdote in connection with this play is to the effect that the playing of Cupid and Psyche led to an intrigue between the elder Baron and Mlle. (or, as we should say, Madame) Molière, the wife of his benefactor.

Cases in which lovers have played love scenes are, of course, as plentiful as blackberries in dramatic annals ; but it is less easy to find trustworthy evidence that they played them either exceptionally well or

Lekain, *Talma,* *p.* 73

exceptionally ill. Lekain, towards the close of his career, fell madly in love with a lady who was not an actress. Whenever he was to play a love scene he made her take her stand at the wing, and addressed to her the raptures intended by the poet for his heroine. A popular Juliet has told me that an old lady of her acquaintance used to say to her, ' Ah, you young people may be all very well, but I saw Charles Kean and Ellen Tree play Romeo and Juliet the evening before their marriage, and I shall never again see the Balcony Scene done as they did it.' Even supposing the old lady to have been a competent critic, I fear her memory must have deceived her. Mr. and Mrs. Charles Kean, ' by an odd but accidental coincidence,' says their official biographer, played *The Honeymoon* the evening after their marriage. Had they played *Romeo and Juliet* the evening before, the coincidence would have been still more quaint, and he could scarcely have failed to notice it.

Mr. and Mrs. C. Kean

Cole, i. p. 334

Cases are not uncommon in which personal hatred and emulation have added zest to scenes of recrimination and invective. The central incident of Scribe and Legouvé's *Adrienne Lecouvreur* is, if not historical, at least legendary. The Duchesse de Bouillon, who was doing her best· to supplant Adrienne in the affections of the Maréchal de Saxe, happened one evening to be seated in a stage box while her rival was playing Phèdre. The actress saw her, and turning away from her confidant, hurled at the head of the great lady the lines :—

Adrienne Lecouvreur

Lema-zurier, ii. p. 292

> Je sais mes perfidies,
> Œnone, et ne suis point de ces femmes hardies,
> Qui, goûtant dans le crime une tranquille paix,
> Ont su se faire un front qui ne rougit jamais.

The public, it is said, recognised the application, and applauded it. We read of Rachel, too, that in the part of Marie Stuart in Lebrun's tragedy of that

Rachel, Houssaye, p. 151.

name, she played flatly and without inspiration until, in the scene with Elizabeth, she stood face to face with an actress whom a hostile clique were trying to exalt into rivalry with her. Then she suddenly threw off her languor and played the scene with such intensity that the unhappy Elizabeth 'étonnée et confondue, reculait d'épouvante. . . . Ce fut une verve incroyable, une passion qui allait jusqu'au délire.' It swept her rival from her path at once and for ever. These cases of hatred touch our argument more nearly than those of love. Hatred, uttering itself in the form of rage, presents far more active and characteristic external symptoms than belong to any form of the tender passion ; so that a personal predisposition to anger may very well assist and intensify its mimetic presentation.

Among the artists of to-day I find it generally agreed that an extreme dislike for any fellow-actor might, in spite of themselves, influence their playing for ill, whatever might be the supposed relation of their respective characters. One artist, however, pleads guilty to having entered with peculiar gusto into the nightly task of baffling and finally checkmating a fellow-artist of extremely unsympathetic private character ; while, on the other hand, a well-known actor says, ' I never played Claude Melnotte better than to the Pauline of Miss So-and-so, whom I detested.' One or two actresses admit, theoretically, that they would feel constrained and ill at ease in playing Juliet to a Romeo who stood to them in a nearer relation than one of ordinary esteem and courtesy. It would seem like wearing their heart upon their sleeve, and making a show of the sanctities of life. But, with a few reservations and exceptions, the general answer to this question is that personal feeling towards a fellow-artist makes but little difference, while the fellow-artist's talent and earnestness make all the difference in the world. I add earnestness, because talent, though the main thing, is not the whole secret. A bad actor, it is said, may sometimes be easy to play to, and a good actor difficult. I have been much struck by a remark of Miss Alma Murray's, to the effect that in playing to an actor who is languid and uninterested one is forced, in order to keep oneself up to the emotion of the scene, mentally to act the other part as well, of course at the cost of great exertion. Diderot's clockwork actor would certainly have the advantage of being exempt from this necessity.

Miss Alma Murray

In sum, then, there is no reason to deny that lovers have often played love-scenes well (though according to Diderot, they had no business to do so), and still less can we doubt that real love has often grown out of the mimic passion of the scene. But whereas it is evident that personal sorrow may, and often does, lend exceptional truth and intensity to mimic pathos, there is no convincing proof that personal love ever reinforces, in any perceptible degree, the utterance of stage-love. And the reason is—pardon the reiteration—that love, unlike sorrow, has no simple and characteristic physical expression to which the nerve-centres require to be attuned.

H

CHAPTER VI.

THE LIFE SCHOOL.

LET us now compare with personal emotion revived by the mimic situation, that 'emotion recollected in tranquillity' of which some great artists are known to have made use. Talma is the classic case in point. 'A peine oserai-je dire,' he says, 'que moi-même dans une circonstance de ma vie où j'éprouvai un chagrin profond, la passion du théâtre était telle en moi, qu'accablé d'une douleur bien réelle, au milieu des larmes que je versais, je fis malgré moi une observation rapide et fugitive sur l'altération de ma voix et sur une certaine vibration spasmodique qu'elle contractait dans les pleurs ; et, je le dis non sans quelque honte, je pensais machinalement à m'en servir au besoin ; et en effet cette expérience sur moi-même m'a souvent été très-utile.' M. Coquelin states, on I know not what authority, that this 'circumstance' in Talma's life was the death of his father.

In scenes of emotion in real life, whether you are a parti-cipant in them (e.g. the death-bed of a relative) or a casual on-looker (e.g. a street accident), do you consciously note effects for subsequent use on the stage? Or can you ever trace an effect used on the stage to some phase of such a real-life experi-ence automatically registered in your memory?

Talma,

Réflexions sur Lekain, p. 74

L'Art et le Comédien, p. 27.

I have been told of Rachel (but have failed to find the authority for the anecdote) that one of her greatest effects in Corneille's *Horace* was studied from life. Overhearing a chance conversation one day, she learned of the unexpected death of a dear friend. She uttered a cry, and staggered half-fainting to a chair ; but at the same moment it struck her that this was the very tone and action required for the cry of 'Hélas!' when Camille learns of the death of her lover. She studied and rehearsed the passage in this new light, making it one of her most famous effects.

'I have seen in Mrs. Siddons,' says Boaden, 'hundreds of touches caught by herself from the real world—

> She is a great observer, and she looks
> Quite through the deeds of men.

It is commonly deemed no slight ordeal to have her steady gaze bent upon you, as she sits, too willingly, silent a long time in society. Nor is this the result of prudence or reserve, for she has a sound understanding, and is well read—it is her choice : to *observe* is her mental discipline.' 'Kean,' writes Alfred Bunn, 'sat up all night in a room opposite the Debtor's Door of the Old Bailey, to catch a full view of the deaths of the Cato Street conspirators ; and as he was going on the stage in the evening, he said to me, " I mean to die like Thistlewood to-night ; I'll imitate every muscle of that man's countenance." ' Macready told Lady Pollock that he 'once in a dream saw and heard definitely and distinctly a friend lately dead, who came to address to him words of admonition.

Rachel

Mrs. Siddons, Life of Mrs. Siddons, ii. p. 180

E. Kean, Bunn, ii. p. 208

Macready, Macready as I knew him, p. 11

He woke in extraordinary emotion, and the image of this man filled his mind for long afterwards. Whenever he was to act Hamlet, he summoned up the *Remi-niscences, i. p. 105* passion of that dream.' Macready himself relates that the recollection of a prisoner on trial at Carlisle 'vainly attempting to preserve his composure under the consciousness of guilt' greatly aided him in 'giving reality to the emotion of the agonised Mentevole' in Jephson's *Julia, or the Italian Lover.* Studies *Remi-niscences, i. p. 188* of madness are very common. Macready, when quite a young man, visited an asylum in Glasgow, and 'took from thence,' he says, 'lessons . . . that in after years added to the truth of my representations.' Again, *Remi-niscences, i. p. 344* when preparing to play Lear, he notes in his diary (August 31, 1832), 'Went to Bedlam. . . . Nerves not *Fru Win-terhjelm* able to bear it ; came away.' Fru Hedvig Winterhjelm, one of the leading actresses of Scandinavia, tells me that she has gone through a systematic study of madness, and has been 'struck by the few and slight touches required to produce the most terrible *Miss Ellen Terry* effects.' Miss Ellen Terry, before her first performance of Ophelia, payed a long visit to Banstead Asylum.

Many actors deny that they ever note the effects upon themselves or others of moments of high excitement. *Mr. Bouci-cault* ment. 'I am not so cold-blooded,' writes Mr. Dion Boucicault ; and several other artists answer to the same effect. The majority of my informants, however, admit that the actor's habit of mind prompts him, as he goes through life, to seize upon and treasure up details which may be of use in his art ; though this seems often to occur without any distinct act of will.

'A thousand times,' writes Salvini, 'I have availed myself of emotions experienced in real life, adapting them to the personage and situation.' 'Malgré moi,' M. Albert Lambert writes, 'quelle que soit la douleur que j'éprouve, je vois tous, j'entends tout, je note tout, et cela ne diminue pas mon émotion. On n'a pas qu'une case dans le cerveau. Il me semble que cela doit arriver à tout le monde, à moins d'avoir un cerveau incomplet.' 'There have been events,' writes Mrs. Bancroft, 'which have so impressed me that when opportunity offered I have reproduced them.' 'As a casual onlooker,' writes Miss Isabel Bateman, 'I have noted effects of real emotion, and stored them up for possible use.' Mr. Lionel Brough holds that 'all scenes in real life are impressed on the mind of the real actor, and if occasion requires he will try to reproduce them.' Mr. John Drew, the excellent light comedian of Daly's company, writes as follows : 'I have consciously noted facts in real life for future use, but have never yet had opportunity to put them in practice. I have been able, however, to trace effects made to certain incidents automatically registered in my memory, though at the time of using them I fancied them imaginary or invented.' Miss Dorothy Dene is conscious of studying effects of real emotion in which she herself participates ; 'but,' she adds, 'it is quite against my will.' Similarly, Miss Janet Achurch writes : 'It is impossible for me to help it. Everything that comes, or ever has come, into my own life, or under my observation, I find myself utilising ; and in scenes of

Salvini

M. Lambert

Mrs. Bancroft

Miss Isabel Bateman

Mr. Lionel Brough

Mr. John Drew

Miss Dorothy Dene

Miss Achurch

real personal suffering I have had an under-consciousness of taking mental notes all the time. It is not a pleasant feeling.' 'I often trace an effect used on the stage,' Miss Maud Milton writes, 'to some real experience of my own automatically registered in my memory. I think, she adds—and the remark is most suggestive—'that good works of fiction by students of human nature have a great influence on our conception of stage-character and on our methods of expressing emotion.' If this be so (and it seems highly probable) one cannot but wonder whether the faults of some actors may not be due to false conceptions of life and nature gathered from bad works of fiction.

Miss Maud Milton

Lastly, let me cite a remarkable instance in which a casual but very impressive real-life experience has been utilised on the stage—as my informant believes, with good effect. 'In the streets of Cardiff,' writes Mr. Leonard Boyne, 'I once saw an Italian stab another fatally. I was on the opposite side of the road, and I gave a yell or scream and rushed to take the knife. That incident is always vividly before my eyes when I see Tybalt stab Mercutio; and I have ever since, when playing Romeo, used the "yell." I have noticed a dead silence come over the house immediately, as if something beyond mere acting had happened. One of the audience told me the scream was so effective that he thought the man was actually stabbed, and he was completely carried away by the scene.' This seems at first sight like a perfect example of 'emotion recollected in tranquillity.' But can Mr.

Mr. Leonard Boyne

Boyne reproduce the cry, with certainty of effect, in perfectly cold blood? Does he not depend upon the emotional tension of the scene to attune him for the effort? I confess to a doubt whether Talma (who explicitly rejects Diderot's theory) could reproduce in perfect tranquillity the 'spasmodic vibration' of voice which he originally owed to overmastering emotion. There is nothing in his own account of the matter to show that he could. Even the poet, though he seldom writes under the first stress of passion or pain, must summon up a certain 'fine frenzy' before he can recollect, or, as Mr. Browning would say, 'recapture,' his grief or rapture. As the *Westminster* reviewer aptly puts it, 'What comes of being entirely tranquil, let the bulk of Wordsworth's own verse testify.'

Réflexions sur Lekain, p. 40

What, then, is the upshot of this part of our inquiry? There can be no doubt that emotional experience, and the study of emotion in others, are of the greatest value to actors. If this were not so, the mimetic art would not be mimetic. Even those of my informants who deny this are probably more dependent than they think on the unconscious action of their memory in registering real-life effects. Has not M. Sarcey recently been lamenting the passing away of the good old days of histrionic Bohemianism, urging that in their present state of domesticated respectability, actors and actresses are too much exempt from those crises of passion and rapture and despair which are necessary to the perfecting of their art? But whereas there is ample evidence of the tendency of personal feeling to mingle with scenic emotion of

similar quality—as the vibration of one string will
induce sympathetic vibrations in another tuned to the
same pitch—there is comparatively little evidence of
a tendency to store up in the memory particular
ebullitions of personal emotion, and no evidence
whatever that these ebullitions can be convincingly
reproduced in cold blood. This the anti-emotionalists
must prove—or rather they must prove that the
ebullitions cannot be convincingly reproduced except
in cold blood—before the case of Talma avails them
one iota.

CHAPTER VII.

THE PASSION OF LAUGHTER.

JOY, in the civilised adult at any rate, has no such immediate and characteristic expression as grief or terror. The most stoical among us will scarcely receive a crushing blow without exhibiting some outward sign of dejection; but the best of good tidings (after, perhaps, a single exclamation of surprise) will hardly ruffle our outward calm. A state of high spirits, however, has certain characteristic symptoms, the chief of which is a proneness to laughter. According to Darwin, 'Laughter seems primarily to have been the expression of mere joy or happiness'; and though it has become in a measure specialised as the expression of that complex emotion which we term amusement, it still, to some extent, fulfils its primary function. There is, therefore, a just instinct in the popular antithesis of 'laughter and tears' as the characteristic expressions of joy and grief. Having inquired into the tendency of imagined sorrow to affect the physical organism, I was anxious similarly to test the action of imagined joy, and in order to do so I was compelled to treat laughter as its proper expression. At the same time, overestimating,

Expression of the Emotions, p. 198

perhaps, the degree in which laughter has become specially associated with amusement, I conceived that to treat it as a general manifestation of high spirits would lead to misunderstanding; consequently I framed my questions thus :—

In scenes of laughter (for instance, Charles Surface's part in the Screen Scene, or Lady Teazle's part in the quarrel with Sir Peter), do you feel genuine amusement? Or is your merriment entirely assumed? Have you ever laughed on the stage until the tears ran down your face? or been so overcome with laughter as to have a difficulty in continuing your part? And in either of these cases, what has been the effect upon the audience?

To this section a note was appended explaining that it did not refer to laughter caused by chance blunders or other unrehearsed incidents, but solely to that which forms part of the business of the play.

The answers somewhat surprised me. For reasons to be stated presently, I anticipated that there would be as great a preponderance of testimony against the reality of stage-laughter as for the reality of stage-tears. As a matter of fact, the evidence is pretty evenly balanced, but deflects, if anything, on the side of reality. Were we to include among the affirmative answers those which attribute genuine stage-laughter to the reaction of the spectators' hilarity upon the performer, the 'ayes' would have it by a large majority. Of this class of answer, the following, from Mr. W. H. Vernon, is a good specimen. ' I have often,' he writes, ' felt genuine amusement in a scene, and an exhilaration of spirits caught (doubtless) from an unusually responsive audience, which has visibly reacted and produced the best possible effect. In

Mr. Vernon

comedy the actor is more alive to his audience's humour than in tragedy. The effect is instantaneous, and a good-tempered house evokes the best qualities of a comedian by placing him on good terms with himself.' Many other artists practically echo Mr. Vernon, and must be classed as undecided. Mr. Toole, for example, says, in his recently published *Reminiscences*, ' Yes, I enjoy a rollicking farce. I laugh with the audience, and get carried away by the fun of it.' The contagion of laughter from an appreciative pit must certainly be potent ; so much so, indeed, that one actor tells me he has often had to pinch himself or otherwise inflict physical pain in order to repress this sympathetic hilarity. But it is not the hilarity referred to in my questions. What I wished to ascertain was whether the humour of a laughter-scene, unaided by the enjoyment of the audience, is apt to take such hold upon the player as to make him laugh without any effort of will. The two forms of laughter—laughter from sympathy with the character, and laughter from sympathy with the audience—must always tend to coalesce ; yet I believe that an observant artist must be able, up to a certain point, to distinguish between them.

Mr. Toole

' To me,' writes Signor Salvini, ' it is more difficult to compass mirth than sorrow. I have almost always wept from real grief upon the stage, but I have never laughed with conscious enjoyment. And in truth my simulated laughter has never transfused itself into the audience, which has remained insensible to my gaiety.' There is nothing surprising in this confes-

Salvini

sion, unless it be its frank simplicity; and that can
surprise .none but those who insist on regarding
actors, not as serious and self-respecting artists, but
as mere childish and morbidly egoistic triflers. Many
actors who are not, like Salvini, exclusive devotees
of the 'grave cothurnate Muse' agree with him in declaring their own stage-laughter 'an artificial effort.'
Among those who hold this view I may mention Mr.
and Mrs. Kendal, Mr. Boucicault, Mr. Pinero, Mr. John
Drew, and Mr. Wenman—all of them comedians
whose mirth, whether real or assumed, has awakened
thousandfold reverberations in many a crowded
theatre. I have little doubt, however, that even they,
if the point were specially suggested to them, would
allow a certain effect to contagion from the audience.

On the other hand, many witnesses of no less
authority maintain that their laughter is frequently,
if not always, unforced. On such a question no one,
surely, has a better right to be heard than Mrs. John
Wood. 'I am always genuinely amused,' she writes,
'when I act a comic character, and my laughter is
frequently spontaneous. . . . I have noticed that any
point that is made spontaneously always has an
electric effect upon the audience, if it is in perfect
harmony with the scene.' Take, now, the testimony
of Mr. Lionel Brough. 'In playing parts like Tony
Lumpkin, I feel that I *am* Tony Lumpkin, and feel
myself "full of laughter." I don't remember ever
laughing until tears ran down my face, but *with a
good audience* I have laughed and enjoyed myself as
much as if I had been in the real situations.' The

Mrs. John Wood

Mr. Lionel Brough

phrase I have italicised indicates that Mr. Brough
is to some extent dependent on reaction from the
audience. Indeed, this may be taken for granted in
all cases ; though the ideal actor of the anti-emotionalists should by rights be ready, if necessary, to reel off
his thoroughly-mastered lesson before ' a churchyard
full of gravestones '—to quote John Ryder's graphic
description of an irresponsive house. Macready, while
forming his Drury Lane company, wrote to Henry
Compton asking his opinion of a certain light comedian whom he thought of engaging. ' He has some
fun,' replied Compton, ' which I think does not amount
to enjoyment. I never saw him carried away by the
exuberance of his spirits.' Had Macready been a
believer in Diderot, he would have taken this as a
strong recommendation ; but Compton (himself a delightful comedian) clearly designed it as a reproach.
'My heart is as much in laughter as in emotion,' Mrs.
Bancroft writes. ' Without a keen enjoyment of a
comic situation my laughter would be empty—a
hollow imitation. All acting must be an assumption
at the start, but as I grow and advance with the play
I become more and more influenced by its argument,
and therefore more absorbed in it. . . . I *have* laughed
on the stage till I cried, but not as a rule. All
emotions should be guided by discretion, or one would
be in constant hysterics.' As Mrs. Bancroft's irresistible laugh is certainly not the least of her gifts, this
testimony is extremely valuable. Mrs. Bancroft also
tells how Mr. H. J. Byron, who had of course studied
her talent very carefully, could detect in her laughter

Compton,
p. 100

Mrs.
Bancroft

states of feeling of which she herself was scarcely conscious. He would come round after the performance and ask, ' Are you not well to-night?' 'Yes, quite well,' Mrs. Bancroft (then Miss Marie Wilton) would reply. 'There was something the matter with your laugh,' he would say—and on reflection Mrs. Bancroft would admit (what she had before scarcely realised) that some petty annoyance had been preoccupying her mind. So minute are the differences between what is absolutely true in art, and what (to the delicate sense) is perceptibly false !

Mr. Coleman

Mr. John Coleman sends me some interesting notes on this point. He is all for the reality of laughter in such passages as the Screen Scene. ' I have often gone on the stage,' he writes, ' very nervous and depressed, but have forgotten all my troubles by the time I have arrived at the Screen Scene, and have entered thoroughly into the spirit of the thing. I am always physically exhausted at the end of the scene, and a little angry with myself for liking such a cad as Charles proves himself to be in this particular situation.' Mr. Coleman has a curious and very plausible theory as to the origin of the extraordinary ' Kch !' (like the sound of a saw) with which, according to stage tradition, Sir Peter Teazle and Charles Surface accompany the backward jerk of their thumbs to indicate the presence of the little French milliner behind the screen. Mr. Coleman believes that the original Sir Peter and Charles (King and Gentleman Smith) must have been very good laughers and that the absurd sound now considered indispens-

able must have originated in the mechanical imitation
by inferior actors of their explosions of ill-suppressed
merriment.   It is certainly difficult to guess what
sound in nature can have suggested the 'Kch!' of
the traditional Charles.   Mr. Coleman, too, relates
a half-pathetic anecdote to show, as he says, 'how
nearly akin laughter is to hysteria.'   William Farren, | Farren
the celebrated Sir Peter Teazle, Lord Ogleby, and
Grandfather Whitehead, made his last appearance on
the stage at Sheffield, under Mr. Coleman's manage-
ment. 'He had suffered from paralysis of the vocal cord,
so that his articulation was imperfect and frequently
unintelligible.   Notwithstanding, he looked noble and
distinguished, and emitted flashes of his old fire.   His
character was Sir Peter, and the Joseph was a veteran
actor who had been a captain in the army, and had
acted with Kean.   When the two old gentlemen commenced to laugh about the " little French milliner,"
the audience laughed with them at first.   Encouraged
by this, they went on and on till they became quite
hysterical (producing a somewhat similar effect on the
audience) and at last collapsed altogether.   In vain
the prompter prompted ; in vain Lady Teazle urged
them to go on ; deuce a word could they utter, good,
bad, or indifferent, until Charles spoke without, and
sent the servant to get Sir Peter off.'

We must go to France for other instances of
inextinguishable laughter arising out of the business
of the scene.   It is recorded of Mlle. Desmares, on | Mlle.
Desmares,
the authority of Lesage, that she would often interrupt | *Lema-*
the action of a comedy ' pour céder à une folle envie | *zurier, ii.*
p. 162

de rire.' Now Desmares was one of the best sou-
brettes of her time, and so popular that the public
used to applaud even these extravagant accesses of
mirth. M. Lambert père writes :—' Je me suis amusé
pour mon compte beaucoup après m'être bien mis
dans la situation et j'ai réussi, grâce à ce moyen, à
trouver des effets comiques inattendus, maintenu par
cette bonne humeur entraînée et entraînante qui se
communique aussi vivement que le bâillement. Je
dois avouer, pourtant, qu'une fois je me suis pris moi-
même et qu'une idée si burlesque m'empoigna dans
une situation comique dont j'avais tiré de grands effets,
que je ris de telle façon qu'il me fallut quitter la
scène—mais je commençais le théâtre à cette époque
et n'étais pas maître de moi suffisamment.'

Many other artists—I may name Mr. Clayton,
Mr. Beerbohm Tree, Mr. Wilson Barrett, Miss Alma
Murray, Miss Wallis, Mrs. Chippendale, and Miss
Geneviève Ward—believe that stage-laughter is often
genuine ; and this, as I have said, was at first a surprise to me. Every theatre-goer must have noticed
the comparative rarity of good laughter on the stage.
Tolerable pathos is far commoner than even mode-
rately convincing merriment—so it seems to me, at
any rate, and (I find) to many other observers. I
imagined that the explanation of this lay in the very
nature of laughter. Its causes and conditions are still
moot questions, but I found all theorists agree in
regarding suddenness and unexpectedness of impression as an almost essential factor in its production.
Hobbes puts this very strongly in a well-known

passage. 'Forasmuch,' he says, 'as the same Thing is no more ridiculous when it groweth stale or usual, whatever it be that moveth Laughter it must be *new* and *unexpected*. . . . I may therefore conclude that the Passion of Laughter is nothing else but *sudden Glory* arising from a sudden *Conception* of some *Eminency* in ourselves, by *Comparison* with the *Infirmity* of others, or with our own formerly.' This analysis, though obviously incomplete, is generally held to be correct in its insistance on novelty as an important element in the ludicrous. Diggory, indeed, had laughed 'these twenty years' at Mr. Hardcastle's story of the grouse in the gun-room, but it may have been part of 'the constant service of the antique world' to suffer no amount of custom to stale a patron's jest. Now, the jests of the stage, whether they lie in dialogue or in situation, are necessarily familiar to the performer; and in this fact I thought I had found a reason for the infrequency of natural stage-laughter. But the answers I have just summarised show that stage-laughter may be, and often is, perfectly natural, in the sense of being produced by no deliberate simulative effort. Hence I conclude, on the one hand, that merriment retains, in almost unimpaired activity, its original function as a safety-valve for mere high spirits, not necessarily connected with any ludicrous idea; and, on the other hand, that the things which tickle our risible muscles need by no means be 'new and unexpected.' Everyday experience, indeed, is sufficient to show that 'the dearest jokes are the auldest jokes.' Which of us has not

Human Nature, chap. iv. par. 13

I

laughed a hundred times at Falstaff and at Dogberry,
though we may know by heart every word they utter?
Which of us can refrain from laughing when some
passage of arms between Boswell and Johnson flashes
upon the memory—the colloquy about the baby in
the tower, for example? or when we think of Sam
Weller's skirmish with Mr. Justice Stareleigh, or of
Jos Sedley's heroism on the eve of Waterloo? A
few moments ago, some accident recalled to my mind
that sublime translation from Heine's *Wallfahrt nach
Kevlaar* in an Anglo-German guide-book to the
Rhine :—

> Many came hither on crutches
> Who now dance so stealthy,
> Many now play on the viol
> Who formerly were not healthy—

and though it has been a joy to me for years, I laugh
as I write it down.   Age, indeed, is the chief merit of
some witticisms.   We laugh at them because we have
been in the habit of doing so since our childhood ; we
should now be puzzled to say where the humour comes
in.   Why, then, should not a comedian laugh in the
most hackneyed situations?   To an actor of mobile
midriff, it may well be more difficult to restrain
laughter in scenes whose humour depends on his gravity
than to summon it up when the action requires it.   If
this be so, we may probably find an explanation of the
rarity of good laughers on the stage in the simple fact
that good laughers are no less rare in real life.   We all
know men or women who are celebrated for a particularly pleasant or hearty laugh, just as they might be for

any other uncommon physical charm. The ordinary laugh of the ordinary man, if not unpleasant, is apt to be trivial, and a laugh which would not specially annoy us in real life may become exasperating when transported to the stage. Thus, what with unskilfully simulated laughter and unpleasant natural laughter, the merriment of the scene becomes, as a whole, unconvincing. It is only exceptional artists who either simulate laughter to perfection or are happily endowed by nature with musical and infectious glee.

CHAPTER VIII.

NATURE'S COSMETICS.

THE muscles of the throat and even the lachrymal glands are more or less under the control of the will. However strong a probability we may establish, it is impossible absolutely to prove, in any given instance, that tears in the eyes or in the voice are the result of emotion. But can we find no symptoms of emotion which are utterly beyond the control of the will, and cannot possibly be simulated? If such symptoms of real emotion are found commonly to accompany the imagined emotion of the stage, will they not prove a very close analogy, at least, between the two phenomena?

Blushing and pallor precisely fulfil these requirements. If we could hear (for instance) of any Rosalind who blushes at the line 'Alas the day! what shall I do with my doublet and hose?' and turns pale when she hears of Orlando's wound, this would prove a curious degree of what may be called physical identification with the character, for the very reason that the actress could not possibly produce these changes by any voluntary effort. Physiological records may furnish cases of a power to blush and

blench at will; but even if these exist (they have
not come to my knowledge) we can only regard such
a faculty as a freak of nature, much more abnormal
than (for example) the power of moving their ears
which some people possess. I have heard of, and
seen, an instance in which a distinguished actor produces, by a mechanical device, a sudden and very
striking pallor, which is of great value in one particular
situation. But this effect depends upon morbid physical conditions, and does not in the least invalidate
the general principle that changes of colour are beyond the control of the will. In Mr. Gilbert's *Comedy
and Tragedy*, where Clarice breaks off her improvisation in an agony of dread, which is mistaken by the
onlookers for part of her performance, Dr. Choquart
alone exclaims, 'This is not acting. Her colour comes
and goes!' As a medical man, the worthy doctor
knows that these functions of the ' vaso-motor system '
are quite involuntary, and accordingly concludes
(rightly enough, as it happens) that Clarice's agony is
real. But had he examined into the matter a little
more closely, he might not have been so confident.
He would have found that imagined emotion may,
and often does, approach so nearly to reality as to be
accompanied by the very same symptoms, though
probably in a minor degree. Of this the answers
to the following question leave, I think, no possible
doubt :—

Do you ever blush (involuntarily) when representing bashfulness, modesty, or shame? or turn pale in scenes of terror? or
have you observed these physical manifestations in other artists?

On this question I have two remarks to make. The first is, that when I formulated it I had neither read of nor observed cases of blushing and pallor on the stage. I must have come across one or two of the anecdotes to be quoted presently, but they had made no impression upon me. The question was entirely the result of an *a priori* process of reasoning. If my hypothesis as to the nature of mimetic emotion was the true one, these symptoms must certainly accompany it; but when I issued my interrogatory I was unaware of any positive evidence on the point. Thus the emotional theory, as I understand it, led me to a prediction, or rather anticipation, which subsequent inquiry has amply justified.

Secondly, it seems worth while to note that in the original edition of my interrogatory the word 'involuntarily' was omitted, so that this was not a leading but a *mis*leading question. Almost all my informants misunderstood its purpose, and, thinking to contradict my theory, unconsciously confirmed it. Supposing me to refer to voluntary changes of colour, they assured me that no one can blush and turn pale at will, and that at best it would be useless, since the changes would be practically invisible to the audience by reason of the actor's make-up. But the great majority of them (at least three-fourths) added either that they themselves *involuntarily* change colour, or that they have seen others do so; which was precisely the point I aimed at.

First among the witnesses to pallor as a possible effect of mimic emotion, I may place one who, if not a great actor, was at least a competent observer— William Shakespeare, to wit. He tells us how the First Player could

> Force his soul so to his own conceit
> That at her working all his visage wann'd ;

and he evidently thinks no worse of the nameless tragedian for ' feeling his part' to this degree. It is surely not too rash to conjecture that he had seen in Burbage or Alleyn the changes of countenance which he attributes to the 'master' of the strolling company. As to Betterton, unquestionably one of the greatest actors that ever trod the boards, we find it positively averred that he not only changed colour but produced a great effect by so doing. The author of *The Laureat, or, the Right Side of Colley Cibber, Esq.*, writes as follows :—' I have lately been told by a Gentleman who has frequently seen Mr. *Betterton* perform this part of *Hamlet*, that he has observ'd his Countenance (which was naturally ruddy and sanguin) in this Scene of the fourth Act, where his Father's Ghost appears, thro' the violent and sudden Emotions of Amazement and Horror, turn instantly on the Sight of his Father's Spirit, as pale as his Neckcloath, when every Article of his Body seem'd to be affected with a Tremor inexpressible ; so that, had his Father's Ghost actually risen before him, he could not have been seized with more real Agonies ; and this was felt so strongly by the Audience, that the Blood seemed to shudder in their Veins likewise, and they in some Measure partook of the Astonishment and Horror, with which they saw this excellent Actor affected.'

Baron

Dorat,
f. 47

The following anecdote of Baron, the Betterton of France, would be still more valuable if we could altogether believe it ; but I admit that it verges on the marvellous :—' Baron, après sa retraite, qui fut de plus de vingt années, remonta sur la Scène ; elle étoit alors en proie à des Déclamateurs boursoufflés qui mugissoient des vers au lieu de les réciter.   Il débuta par le rôle de *Cinna.*   Son entrée sur le Théâtre, noble, simple et majestueuse, ne fut point goûtée par un Public accoutumé à la fougue des Acteurs du temps ; mais lorsque dans le Tableau de la Conjuration, il vint à ces beaux vers :

> Vous eussiez vu leurs yeux s'enflammer de fureur,
> Et dans un même instant, par un effet contraire,
> Leur front pâlir d'horreur, et rougir de colère,

on le vit pâlir et rougir successivement.   Ce passage si rapide fut senti par les Spectateurs.   La Cabale frémit, et se tût.'   It is possible, to be sure, that the habit of ' forcing his soul to his conceit ' may have begotten in Baron an excessive mobility of the vaso-motor system, placing it, in effect, under the control of his will.   In that case, this particular incident could not be cited as a proof that the actor was, at the moment, under the influence of emotion ; but, on the other hand, such a faculty can only have arisen from the frequency of emotional changes of colour, gene-rating in the vessels of the skin a peculiar, not to say unique, sensitiveness.

The flush of fury is not so directly germane to our argument as the blush of shame, for it can be mechanically produced ; yet the following note upon

Barry's Othello surely does not describe a mere mus-   Barry,
cular forcing of blood to the head :—' When Shake-   *The Actor,*
speare puts in the mouth of his enraged Moor . . .   1755, *p.* 9
this great and soldier-like expression—

> Had all his hairs been lives,
> My great revenge had stomach for them all—

we see Mr. Barry redden through the very black
of his face ; his whole visage becomes inflamed, his
eyes sparkle with successful vengeance, and he
seems to raise himself above the ground while he
pronounces it.'

As to pallor, again, this passage from Davies'
Dramatic Miscellanies is very much to the point ; and   *iii. p.* 58
Davies, let me repeat, had excellent facilities for observation : ' Mrs. Siddons, very lately, in the third   Mrs.
act of the Fair Penitent, was so far affected with   Siddons
assuming the mingled passions of pride, fear, anger,
and conscious guilt, that I might appeal to the spectators, whether, in spite of the rouge which the actress
is obliged to put on, some paleness did not show itself
in her countenance.   I think, too, that Mrs. Cibber,   Mrs.
Mrs. Yates, Mrs. Crawford, and Miss Younge have   Cibber,
Mrs. Yates,
given the same proof of consummate feeling in scenes   &c.
of a similar nature.'

Writing of her first appearance as Juliet, Fanny   Fanny
Kemble tells how the part gradually took possession   Kemble
of her.   In the first scene she was self-conscious and
inaudible ; in the next, the ball-room scene, she began to forget herself ; in the third, the balcony-scene,
she had done so entirely.   ' For aught I knew,' she   *Record of a*
Girlhood,
continues, ' I was Juliet ; the passion I was uttering   *ii. p.* 60

sending hot waves of blushes all over my neck and shoulders, while the poetry sounded like music to me as I spoke it.' Fanny Kemble was then a beginner; but she repeatedly avers that a hot blush always 'bepainted her cheek' in the Balcony Scene. Miss Helen Faucit, one of the most accomplished artists of her day, bears emphatic testimony, not only to the fact of changing colour, but to its artistic value :— 'The abuse of cosmetics on the French stage,' she writes, 'which was then [1845] habitual, has since been carried in many instances to excess upon our own. When the skin is covered with what is, in effect, a painted mask, the colour, which under strong emotion would come and go, is hidden under it, and the natural expression of the countenance destroyed.' Whence proceeds the deadness of a too much made-up face, if not from the suppression of the natural play of colour? Though we may not, as a rule, be actively conscious of its presence, its absence necessarily makes itself felt.

Among the actors of to-day there is little conflict of opinion on the subject of pallor. Salvini's evidence is included in his answer to my first question; but he adds that few actors have the power of so completely entering 'into the skin' of their characters. Ristori declares unhesitatingly that she both blushes and grows pale in accordance with the emotion she is portraying. Many artists who have never observed blushes on the stage have seen lips and cheeks turn white under the make-up, or have been told that their own countenances blench, in scenes of terror. 'I have never

Marginal notes:

Lady Martin

Shakespeare's Female Characters, p. 437

Ante, p. 51

Ristori

known my colour come and go, nor have I ever noticed it in any player,' writes Mr. Forbes Robertson ; and Mr. Dion Boucicault notes with decision, ' No, never —don't believe in it.' These are almost the only thoroughgoing sceptics on the subject of pallor. Others (among whom I may mention Mr. and Mrs. Bancroft and Mr. and Mrs. Kendal) admit that they have noticed it, but regard it as exceptional. Mrs. Kendal remarks that she once produced a very convincing effect of pallor in the Screen Scene in *The School for Scandal,* but as that was due to a mouse running up the back of the screen, it is scarcely a case in point. Many, on the other hand, assert that the 'wanning' of the visage is a common and even habitual accompaniment of imagined terror and kindred emotions. Among these I may name Mr. Clayton, Mr. Beerbohm Tree, Mr. Wilson Barrett, Mr. Augustus Harris, Miss Geneviève Ward, Miss Bateman, Miss Achurch, Miss Dorothy Dene, and Miss Maud Milton. Mr. John Coleman writes, ' I have never known an artist, male or female, accustomed to the higher range of art, who was not subject to these outward manifestations of the inward emotions' ; and an experience of forty years, in close association with most of the leading actors of that period, certainly entitles Mr. Coleman to speak with authority. ' I often turn pale,' writes Miss Isabel Bateman, ' in scenes of terror or great excitement. I have been told this many times, and I can feel myself getting very cold and shivering and pale in thrilling situations.' ' When I am playing rage or terror,' Mr.

Mrs. Kendal

Mr. Coleman

Miss Isabel Bateman

Lionel Brough writes, ' I believe I do turn pale. My mouth gets dry, my tongue cleaves to my palate. . In Bob Acres, for instance (in the last act), I have to continually moisten my mouth or I should become inarticulate. I have to " swallow the lump," as I call it.' This testimony to the effect even of comic terror is extremely curious.

As to blushing, the evidence is less conclusive ; and the reason is not far to seek. Laughter may or may not be 'a passion of sudden glory,' but blushing is certainly an effulgence of sudden shame. A carefully rehearsed humiliation or embarrassment necessarily tends to lose the vividness which whips the blood tingling to the cheeks. Blushing, too, depends on a certain delicacy of the skin which is probably not fostered by the habitual use of cosmetics. Nevertheless, several of my informants allow that they either blush themselves or have seen others blush.

' On the stage,' writes Fru Winterhjelm, ' I blush and turn pale according to the situation. It is therefore my custom to " make up " so lightly as to allow the natural colours to show through ; and this, I have noticed, produces the strongest effect on the audience.' Miss Isabel Bateman, for instance, writes : ' I remember Miss Kate Rorke's blush in *Delicate Ground*—a charming flush that suddenly covered her face, and gave wonderful reality to the scene.' In the few months during which my attention has been specially directed to this point, I have myself noted several unmistakable cases of blushing on the stage. In the third act of *The Railroad of Love*, for example,

I am very much deceived if a warm flush does not overspread Miss Ada Rehan's face at certain points of the boudoir-door scene between Valentine Osprey and Lieutenant Everett.   One case of pallor, too, I witnessed distinctly, and that in no less a person than —M. Coquelin!   It was in the scene in *Les Surprises du Divorce*, in which Henri Duval learns that his hated ex-mother-in-law has, by a horrible freak of fortune, become his step-grandmother-in-law.   M. Coquelin threw into his rendering of this scene an almost tragic intensity, and his pallor at the moment of the awful discovery struck me forcibly.   Still, I should not have ventured to bring it forward in evidence, had not my observation been confirmed by that of another spectator who asked me, without any suggestion on my part, whether I had noticed Coquelin turn pale at that particular point.   Mr. John Drew, again, notes that he has 'known a good effect produced by the sudden, angry flushing of the face after a blow administered on it.'   It might be argued that this flush was a direct result of the blow itself, apart from any emotional process in its recipient ; but if so the buffet must have been unpleasantly realistic.

My next question was simply a following-up of the same line of thought :—

A distinguished actor informs me that he is in the habit of perspiring freely while acting ; but that the perspiration varies, not so much with the physical exertion gone through, as with the emotion experienced.   On nights when he was not 'feeling the part,' he has played Othello 'without turning a hair,' though his physical effort was at least as great as on nights when he was bathed in perspiration.   Does your experience tally with

this? Do you find the fatigue of playing a part directly proportionate to the physical exertion demanded by it? or dependent
on other causes?

The pores of the skin are still more completely
beyond voluntary control than the capillary vessels
which govern the complexion. We are accustomed
to think of perspiration as attendant upon high temperature and violent bodily exertion; but everyone
has also heard of, if not felt, the 'cold sweat' of terror.
A like phenomenon accompanies even the most pas-
sive bodily agony and many other forms of intense

*Expression
of the
Emotions,
p. 73*

feeling. 'When a man suffers from an agony of pain,'
says Darwin, 'the perspiration often trickles down
his face; and I have been assured by a veterinary
surgeon that he has frequently seen drops falling
from the belly, and running down the inside of
the thighs of horses, and from the bodies of cattle,
when thus suffering. He has observed this, when
there has been no struggling which would account for
the perspiration. . . . . So it is with extreme fear;
the same veterinary has often seen horses sweating
from this cause; as has Mr. Bartlett with the rhino-
ceros; and with man it is a well-known symptom.
The cause of perspiration bursting forth in these cases
is quite obscure.' Suppose, then, that an actor plays
the same part on two successive evenings, the temperature and his physical exertion being the same in
both cases: if on the one night he plays mechanically
and without perspiration, while on the other night he
'feels the part' and perspires freely, this fact surely
helps us to understand the precise condition of mind

and body which he designates as 'feeling.' Since mere intellectual exertion has no tendency to produce perspiration, the emotionless actor of Diderot's ideal should perspire in exact proportion to the temperature and to his physical effort. If this is not usually the case, it at least follows that few actors come up to the said ideal.

Unless the point were specially suggested to them, actors would scarcely think of putting on record their experience in this respect. Thus the evidence to be gathered from theatrical biography is meagre. Here, however, is a curiously apt case in point: 'Acted leisurely,' writes Macready (December 6, 1833), '*without inspiration or perspiration*; still, I seemed to produce an effect on the audience, but I was not identified with Werner.' When Henderson first played Hamlet at Bath, says his biographer, he discarded his predecessor's velvet suit and dressed in black cloth. 'Extreme agitation occasioned a perspiration. The coat was wet as if it had been "immersed in the ocean." The performance ended, Hamlet resigned his habit to the keeper of the wardrobe, who received it with astonishment and horror, hung it to the fire, lifted up both hands and exclaimed ". . . Heaven bless us all! . . . They may talk of Muster Lee, and Muster Lee, and Muster Lee, but Muster Lee is nothing to this man—for what they call perspiration." A person present observed that the severest critics must acknowledge the young gentleman had played the character with great warmth, if not with spirit.' There are countless proofs, indeed, of the physical exhaustion attendant upon

Macready *Reminiscences, i.* p. 395

Henderson, *Ireland, p.* 70

Ante, p. 62

*Reminis-
cences, i.
p. 202*

emotional acting.   Mrs. Siddons, for instance, robust
as she was, was frequently prostrated by her bursts
of passion.   As an example, let me quote a curious
account given by Macready of her collapse after playing Arpasia in Rowe's *Tamerlane.* ' In the last act,' he
says, ' when, by order of the tyrant, her lover Monesis
is strangled before her face, she worked herself up to
such a pitch of agony, and gave such terrible reality
to the few convulsive words she tried to utter, as she
sank a lifeless heap before her murderer, that the
audience for a few moments remained in a hush of
astonishment, as if awe-struck ; they then clamoured
for the curtain to be dropped, and insisting on the
manager's appearance, received from him, in answer
to their vehement inquiries, the assurance that Mrs.
Siddons was alive, and recovering from the temporary
indisposition that her exertions had caused. ⹁ They
were satisfied as regarded her, but would not suffer
the performance to be resumed.   As an instance of
the impression this great actress made on individuals
who might be supposed insensible, from familiarity,
to the power of acting, Holman turned to my father,
when Mrs. Siddons had fallen, and looking aghast
in his face, said : " Macready, do I look as pale as
you ? " ' It is incredible that Mrs. Siddons in this
instance was acting in cold blood, or that her exhaustion was due to the mere physical and intellectual
effort of playing Arpasia, who appears in only three
acts out of the five.

Among contemporary artists I find a more general
agreement on the point suggested by this question

than on almost any other. I may even say that all my informants, with one exception, who have had much experience of emotional parts are absolutely unanimous. 'One is never so exhausted as when acting well,' says Mr. Bancroft. 'Playing with the brain,' says Miss Alma Murray, 'is far less fatiguing than playing with the heart. An adventuress taxes the physique far less than a sympathetic heroine. Muscular exertion has comparatively little to do with it.' 'On a bitterly cold night in America,' writes Mr. Wilson Barrett, 'when the thermometer has been 15° below zero, and I have stood shivering at the wings waiting for my entrance in Hamlet, I have been in a profuse perspiration before I had half finished a scene.' 'Emotion while acting,' writes Mr. Howe, 'will induce perspiration much more than physical exertion. I always perspired profusely while acting Joseph Surface, which requires little or no exertion.' Similarly, Mr. Herbert Standing writes, 'I have had the honour of playing in *The Man of the World* with the late Samuel Phelps, and have seen him, while sitting quietly in his chair, bathed in perspiration.' 'Emotion and perspiration,' says Salvini, 'go together. There are characters which call for scarcely any physical exertion, and which are nevertheless most fatiguing: for example the part of Corrado in *La Morte Civile*.' 'Ce qui brise,' says M. Albert Lambert —and this is the one opinion that runs counter to my argument—' ce sont les colères non pensées, les cris froids, les déclamations oiseuses, à côté du sujet et en dehors de la nature.' That these should be very

Marginal notes: Mr. Bancroft · Miss Alma Murray · Mr. Wilson Barrett · Mr. Howe · Phelps · Salvini · Mr. Lambert

K

fatiguing to the actor, as well as to the audience, is comprehensible enough ; but M. Lambert further remarks that by keeping 'le cœur chaud, la tête froide' the actor escapes exhaustion. 'I suffer from

Mr. Forbes Robertson

fatigue,' writes Mr. Forbes Robertson, 'in proportion to the amount of emotion I may have been called upon to go through, and not from physical exertion.'

Mr. Clayton

Mr. Clayton told me that after playing Hugh Trevor, a part which demands no unusual muscular strain, he has been so exhausted that he has lain down on the floor of his dressing-room and said to his dresser, 'Don't come near me for an hour!' feeling as though

Mr. Coleman

he had been thrashed all over. 'Though I have played Othello,' writes Mr. Coleman, 'ever since I was seventeen (at nineteen I had the honour of acting the Moor to Macready's Iago), husband my resources as I may, this is the one part, the part of parts, which always leaves me physically prostrate. I have never been able to find a pigment that would stay on my face, though I have tried every preparation in existence. Even the titanic Edwin Forrest told me that he was always knocked over in Othello, and I have heard Charles Kean, Phelps, Brooke, Dillon, say the same thing. On the other hand I have frequently acted Richard III. without turning a hair.' It is evident that the exceptionally exhausting quality of Othello does not lie in the physical effort it demands. Hamlet, Macbeth, and Richard III. must at least equal it in that. On the other hand, I think we can have no difficulty in recognising a peculiar poignancy in the emotions of 'the great brute gladiator' as Mr. Traill

calls him, 'fast in the toils of Iago Retiarius,' which
(according to my theory) amply explains the overwhelming effect. More than any other of the great
Shakespearean characters (except perhaps King Lear)
Othello must be played with the heart rather than the
head. His head, in truth, was not his strong point.

One or two of my informants are inclined to
attribute perspiration and consequent fatigue to general nervousness rather than to the special emotion
of a particular character. They dwell on the fact
that the nervous excitement of a first night is a noted
sudorific. This argument would be of great weight
if the symptom were confined to first nights and
other peculiarly nervous occasions. But we have no
reason for supposing that the actor referred to in my
question—Mr. Hermann Vezin—was more nervous   Mr. Vezin
one night than another ; unless, indeed, we choose to
argue in a circle and describe as 'nervousness' the
very condition of mind and body which enables a
player to enter into the emotions of his part. It is
true that some great actors have confessed to feeling
a certain nervousness, amounting almost to stage-
fright, every time they faced the public ; but they
have always added that, the first plunge once over,
this sensation passes off. We may readily admit
that nervousness (in the ordinary sense of the term)
heightens the tendency to perspiration on special
occasions ; but it cannot account for the whole phenomenon.

The following observation of François Riccoboni's   F. Ricco-
may be quoted as the most plausible anti-emotionalist   boni

K 2

L'Art du
Théâtre
(1750), p. 41

argument on this point which has come under my notice :—' Je ne dis pas qu'en jouant les morceaux de grande passion l'Acteur ne ressente une émotion très-vive, c'est même ce qu'il y a de plus fatiguant au Théâtre.   Mais cette agitation vient des efforts qu'on est obligé de faire pour peindre une passion que l'on ne ressent pas, ce qui donne au sang un mouvement extraordinaire auquel le Comédien peut être lui-même trompé, s'il n'a pas examiné avec attention la véritable cause d'où cela provient.'   Unless this chapter has entirely failed in its purpose, I think it establishes a fair probability that ' the comedian ' may be right in his self-analysis, and Riccoboni wrong.

' But hold ! ' say the anti-emotionalists, shifting their ground to what may be called Diderot's second position ; ' we do not deny that some, many, even most actors may exhibit symptoms of emotion which cannot be mechanically simulated.   Our point is that the greatest artists do not feel on the stage, and would not be great if they did.'   Then Betterton, Baron, Mrs. Siddons, and Salvini must be relegated to ' the ruck of middling actors '?   That were a paradox indeed.

CHAPTER IX.

'AUTOSUGGESTION' AND 'INNERVATION.'

'I HATE to dissemble when I need not,' says Gatty to her sister Ariana in Etherege's *She Would if She Could*; ''twould look as affected in us to be reserved now we are alone, as for a player to maintain the character she acts in the tiring-room.' Madam Gatty was an anti-emotionalist by instinct. She had not considered whether it be necessary or desirable for the player to attain and preserve a certain emotional level before and during the performance of an arduous part. It is to this point that the following groups of questions refer :—

G. H. Lewes relates how Macready, as Shylock, used to shake a ladder violently before going on for the scene with Tubal, in order to get up 'the proper state of white heat' ; also, how Liston was overheard 'cursing and spluttering to himself, as he stood at the side scene waiting to go on in a scene of comic rage.' Have you experienced any difficulty in thus 'striking twelve at once'? If so, how do you overcome it?

It used to be said of a well-known actor that he put on in the morning the character he was to play at night ; that on days when he was to play Richard III. he was truculent, cynical, and cruel, while on days when he was to play Mercutio or Benedick he would be all grace, humour, and courtesy. Are you conscious of any such tendency in yourself? or have you observed it in others? In the green-room, between the acts, have you any tendency to preserve the voice and manner of the character you are playing? or have you observed such a tendency in others?

Macready and Liston, it may be said, could not affect their emotional states by shaking a ladder and spluttering, these being merely mechanical devices for producing extreme muscular mobility. This argument, however, ignores the undoubted tendency of *Expression of the Emotions, p. 366* outward expression to react upon emotion. ' He who gives way to violent gestures,' says Darwin, ' will increase his rage ; he who does not control the signs of fear will experience fear in a greater degree. . . . Even the simulation of an emotion tends to arouse it *Philosophie des Schönen (1887)* in our minds.' Eduard von Hartmann, ' the Philosopher of the Unconscious,' gives to this principle the hybrid name of ' autosuggestion ' and treats it as one of the central secrets of acting. Lessing too, though he would probably have rebelled at the word, was familiar with the thing. He discusses in his *Ham-* *May 8, 1767* *burgische Dramaturgie* the respective merits of the actor who has feeling (Empfindung) but little power of expression, and the actor who has great power of expression but no feeling. The latter he declares, very naturally, to be the more useful of the two. By merely imitating the emotional expression of others ' he will attain to a sort of feeling, in virtue of the law that those modifications of the soul which produce certain changes of the body, can, conversely, be produced through the medium of these changes. This sort of feeling cannot, certainly, have the persistence and fire of that which takes its rise in the soul ; yet in the moment of performance it is powerful enough to bring about in some measure those involuntary physical changes from whose presence we can alone infer with certainty the presence of the inward emotion. Suppose that such an actor has to express the utmost fury of wrath, and suppose that he does not even understand his part sufficiently to know the reason of this fury. . . . If he has merely learnt to imitate correctly the most obvious symptoms of rage as expressed by an actor of native feeling—the hasty tread, the stamping foot, the rough voice, now screaming, now choking, the play of the eyebrows, the quivering lips, the grinding teeth—if he can imitate these things correctly, I say (and that may be done by a mere effort of will), then a dim feeling of wrath will infallibly seize upon his soul, which, in turn, will react upon his body and produce those changes which do not depend upon our will alone. . . . In short, he will appear to be really enraged, when in truth he is nothing of the sort, and does not even understand " the motive and the cue for passion."' Lessing, I need scarcely point out, was a thorough-going emotionalist.

This principle of ' autosuggestion ' explains Macready's practice, and the similar devices of other actors. It is of course conceivable that Macready may have kept his mind perfectly calm while he worked up the muscular tremor of fury ; but the supposition is difficult. The most intimate correlations can by practice be overcome, just as a juggler can keep five balls in the air with his right hand while with his left he plays

'Home, sweet Home' upon the concertina. Diderot would tell us that Macready ought to have performed a similar feat, but there is no evidence that he did

Expression of the Emotions, p. 116

perform it. 'There is reason to suspect,' says Darwin again, 'that the muscular system requires some short preparation, or some degree of innervation, before being brought into strong action.' Macready's primary object, no doubt, was to mobilise his muscles, but he probably knew very well that in doing so he mobilised his mind.

There is abundant testimony to the difficulty of 'striking twelve at once,' and many methods of overcoming it are on record. It is recorded of Baron that

Baron

before going on the stage in a scene of high excitement, 'il se battait les flancs pour se passionner ; il

Diction-naire Larousse, art. 'Baron'

apostrophait avec aigreur et injuriait tous ceux qui se présentaient à lui, valets et camarades de l'un et de l'autre sexe, et il appelait cela " respecter le parterre."' Sticotti states the same fact in a different form.

Garrick, ed. 1770, *p.* 63

'Baron dans la coulisse,' he says, 'se pénétroit déjà des choses qu'il alloit dire ; il paroissoit hors de lui-même ; il s'interrogeoit, il gémissoit, il parloit aux autres de sa triste situation, comme si elle eût été bien véritable, et dans cet état, il entroit sur la scène ; ce principe excellent est peu suivi des Acteurs médiocres.' This was practically the system of Macready ; and theatrical tradition tells of an actor-manager who carried the same method to a length which neither Baron nor Macready thought necessary. When going on in a particular situation of great excitement, he used to work himself up by kicking the property-man ; it being understood that he should afterwards apologise and give the fellow a shilling. One night, when the house was very bad, the property-man planted himself at the wing to receive the accustomed kicking ; but the canny actor-manager restrained himself, saying as he passed him by, ' Not to-night, Barkins ; the treasury won't stand it.' This gentleman's respect for the property-man varied in the inverse ratio of his respect for the pit.

Many of my informants admit that, though they do not shake ladders or kick property-men, they adopt mechanical means of less violence in order to work themselves up before an excited entrance. They mumble to themselves through their clenched teeth, snap their fingers, hold up their hands and shake them rapidly with a loose wrist, or ' stand rigidly and rock the body to and fro with gradually increasing nerve-tension.' Mr. Arthur Cecil informed me that Phelps used always to stand muttering to himself before making his entrance. One night, during the run of *The Merry Wives of Windsor* at the Gaiety, Phelps lost his way in the intricate passages between his dressing-room and the stage, and was not to be found when his cue was given. The ' wait' was becoming noticeable, when Mr. George Belmore, who happened to be standing at the wing, bethought him to imitate the muttered thunder which used to announce the actor's approach. He thus kept the audience in the belief that the delay was an intentional effect, until the missing Falstaff was rescued from the labyrinth. In hand-to-hand combats such as the death-struggle

Phelps

Phelps and
Macready

of Macbeth or of Richard, tragedians have been
known to hurl the most horrible curses at each other
under their breath.   When Phelps first encountered
Macready on the battlements of Dunsinane, he was
astonished to hear the older tragedian overwhelm
him with savage obloquy.   Thinking that no offence
he could possibly have committed could justify such
treatment, he responded in kind, and 'gave as good
as he got.'   Great was his surprise when, at the end
of the play, Macready thanked him cordially for the
spirited way in which he had played up to him in

Mounet
and
Tessandier,
*Revue
d'Art
Drama-
tique,
March* 1,
1887

the combat.   In a recent revival of Dumas's *Antony*,
Paul Mounet and Madame Tessandier had recourse
to this device : ' Ils avaient intercalé dans une scène
des jurons, des injures que le public n'entendait pas,
mais avec lesquels ils se fouettaient les nerfs ; ils
emportèrent la scène dans un mouvement de passion
échevelée qui électrisa la salle.'   There is a passage in
Rob Roy where the bold outlaw, captured and pinioned,
stands writhing and foaming at the mouth, while the
other characters on the stage are singing the ' Tramp

Mr. J. B.
Howard

Chorus.'   In this scene Mr. J. B. Howard, the Rob
Roy of the modern Scotch stage, was in the habit
of indulging in such copious expletives, that an old
dresser in the Edinburgh Theatre Royal, who used to
be sent on among the 'supers,' begged Mrs. Wyndham
to assign her a place on the stage as far as possible
from Rob Roy, ' for the language he used made her
flesh creep.'   Since then, Mr. Howard has learnt to
do his swearing in Italian.

     As a rule, however, mental concentration, rather

than any physical device, is resorted to in order to overcome the difficulty of 'striking twelve at once.' A favourite and of course a very obvious method is to stand at the wing and drink in every word of the dialogue leading up to the difficult entrance, in order to become impregnated with the spirit of the situation. This was the method adopted by Mrs. Siddons, as she herself tells us in a very curious study of the character of Constance in *King John* :—' . . . If the representative of *Constance*,' she writes, ' shall ever forget, even behind the scenes, those disastrous events which impel her to break forth into the overwhelming effusions of wounded friendship, disappointed ambition, and maternal tenderness, upon the first moment of her appearance in the third Act, when stunned with terrible surprise she exclaims,—

Mrs.
Siddons

Campbell,
i. p. 213

> Gone to be married—gone to swear a peace !
> False blood to false blood joined—gone to be friends !

if, I say, the mind of the actress for one moment wanders from these distressing events, she must inevitably fall short of that high and glorious colouring which is indispensable to the painting of this magnificent portrait. . . . Whenever I was called upon to personate the character of *Constance*, I never, from the beginning of the play to the end of my part in it, once suffered my dressing-room door to be closed, in order that my attention might constantly be fixed on these distressing events which, by this means, I could plainly hear going on upon the stage, the terrible effects of which progress were to be represented by me. Moreover, I never omitted to place myself, with

Arthur in my hand, to hear the word, when, upon the reconciliation of England and France, they enter the gates of Angiers to ratify the contract of marriage between the *Dauphin* and the *Lady Blanche* ; because the sickening sounds of that march would usually cause the bitter tears of rage, disappointment, betrayed confidence, baffled ambition, and, above all, the agonizing feelings of maternal affection, to gush into my eyes. In short, the spirit of the whole drama took possession of my mind and frame, by my attention being incessantly riveted to the passing scenes. . . . I have no doubt that the observance of such circumstances, however irrelevant they may appear upon a cursory view, were [*sic*] powerfully aidant in the representations of those expressions of passion in the remainder of this scene, which have been only in part considered.' It is perhaps worth noting that in the Tubal scene, to which the anecdote of Macready refers, no such process of 'abstraction,' as Mrs. Siddons calls it, is possible, Shylock's entrance following immediately upon a few words of trivial conversation between Salanio and Salarino. Mrs. John Wood writes as follows :—' I once had a lesson that taught me the value of this concentration of mind, and I have never forgotten it. The character I was playing was a wild, uncouth, ragged creature, who was devoted to the villain of the piece, he being the only person who had ever bestowed upon her a kindly thought. For this he became her idol. She watched his words and footsteps, and aided him innocently in his acts of villainy. At last she fancies that he loves the heroine,

Mrs. John Wood

and, in her jealousy, imagines his love returned. She follows him ; he meets the lady of his love ; and she overhears him pour forth his passion. She does not wait to hear the heroine's reply, but rushes at her like a very tigress. The audience waited breathlessly for this supreme moment of the girl's fury, and the scene ended in a most pathetic manner, the sympathy of the public being greatly excited on this poor creature's behalf. I used conscientiously to listen to the preceding scene, and by so doing was really worked up to the right pitch of excitement when my cue came. One night, several of the company, convulsed with laughter, took off my attention by telling me of a great joke they were going to play off upon an unfortunate actor in the next piece. This thoughtlessness ruined my scene. I could not act up to the situation. I did not *feel* it. No amount of art can make up for the want of one real touch of nature. I then found out that they must be *combined* to produce an electrical effect upon your audience.' Miss Ellen Wallis, who has certainly done more than any other living actress to keep alive in the provinces the traditions of poetic drama, instances Isabella's entrance in the last act of *Measure for Measure* as a case in which she has found great difficulty in 'striking twelve at once.' Like Mrs. Siddons, she stations herself at the wing and listens intently to the opening speeches of the scene— the Duke's compliments to Angelo—thus working up her indignation for the great outburst of ' Justice, O royal Duke !' with which she flings herself at his feet. The effort of concentrating the attention is sometimes

Miss Wallis

no less valuable in lowering than in heightening the

Mrs. Kendal

vitality. Mrs. Kendal tells me that, in order to induce in the lines of her face, and in her whole person, the stony rigidity of Claire in *The Ironmaster*, she has often shut herself up in her dressing-room and deliberately fixed her mind upon all the 'old, unhappy, far-off things' she could think of—the pains, losses, and

Mr. Bancroft

disappointments of her life. Mr. Bancroft makes a similar statement with regard to the part of Orloff in *Diplomacy*. He used to prepare himself for the great 'scene of the three men' by the very process em

Miss Ward

ployed by Mrs. Kendal. Miss Geneviève Ward, again, writes :—'I find no difficulty in "striking twelve at once" in passionate or mirthful scenes ; but before death-scenes I wish to be some time alone. My vitality is so strong that for quiet scenes I need to get my nerves under complete control.'

On the other hand we have anecdotes (though I can find but few) of great actors whose extraordinary natural mobility of mind and body enabled them to perform astonishing feats in the way of 'striking twelve at once.' A noteworthy instance is related by

Talma
L'Art et le Comédien,
p. 25

M. Coquelin. 'Talma,' he says, 'jouait Hamlet un soir. En attendant son tour, il causait dans la coulisse avec un ami ; l'avertisseur le voit souriant, distrait, s'approche :—" Monsieur Talma, cela va être à vous !" —" C'est bien, c'est bien, j'attends ma réplique." Sa scène, la scène du spectre, devait commencer dans la coulisse même et le spectateur entendre Talma avant de le voir. Il continue sa causerie, très-gai, la réplique arrive, il serre la main de son interlocuteur, et, le sourire encore aux lèvres, cette main amicale dans la sienne,

> . . . . *Fuis, spectre épouvantable !*

et l'ami recule, effaré, et le frisson tombe dans la salle ! '
Garrick, in private society, would often give the Dagger *Garrick*
Soliloquy from *Macbeth* at a moment's notice. It
is reported of Kean and of Rachel that they would
at one moment be laughing and joking behind the
scenes, and at the next moment on the stage, raving
with Lear or writhing with Phèdre ; while they had
equal facility in stilling the ground-swell of passion at
the end of a trying scene.   Even of Mrs. Siddons Sir *Mrs.*
Walter Scott relates a similar story.   In a drawing- *Siddons*
room one day, wishing to illustrate a peculiarity in
John Philip Kemble's manner, she placed herself in
the attitude of an Egyptian statue—her knees together, her feet turned a little inward, her elbows close
to her sides, her hands folded and held upright with
the palms pressed together—and in this attitude
'proceeded to recite the curse of King Lear on his *Scott, i. p.*
undutiful offspring in a manner which made hair rise *813*
and flesh creep.'   On the other hand, it is said of
Salvini (who, by the way, speaks strongly of the ne- *Salvini*
cessity for ' innervation ') that during a visit to America
he was asked one evening to give a short scene from
the last act of *Othello*, but refused, on the ground that
' it would be impossible for him to present it acceptably *The Voice,*
without going through the entire play.' *x. No. 3*
    I need scarcely say that none of my informants
confesses to ' putting on in the morning the character
he is to play at night.'   That is simply a joke current

among the supporters of a certain tragedian, who, unhappily, played Richard too often for their comfort.

Mossop, *Doran*, ii. *p.* 353
There is a similar legend about Mossop, who was said to 'order his dinner according to the part he had to act : sausages and Zanga, rump-steaks and Richard, pork-chops and Pierre, veal cutlets and Barbarossa.' The same practice is attributed, on his own authority,

Mr. Walter Lacy
to Mr. Walter Lacy, an actor of some eminence in his day, who has now retired from the stage. 'Speaking

Bancroft, i. p. 421
of some of his own performances,' says Mr. Bancroft, 'he thus related his different methods of dining : " When I played Bluff Hall, sir (Henry of England), I drank brown porter and dined off British beef ; but if I had to act the Honourable Tom Shuffleton, I contented myself with a delicate cutlet and a glass of port which resembled a crushed garnet, and then sallied on to the stage with the manners of a gentleman and the devil-me-care air of a man about town ! "' This method of tempering the gastric juices might be indefinitely refined upon. Mr. Irving ought to dine on devilled kidneys before playing Mephistopheles. When *Macbeth* is in the bill, haggis should reek on the tragedian's board, and hasty-pudding should put him i' the vein for Lear.

But if no one 'puts on in the morning the character he is to play at night,' almost everyone who

Macready, *Reminiscences*, i. p. 115
is accustomed to highly emotional or even strongly marked characters admits the desirability of (so to speak) keeping the thread unbroken from first to last. 'My long experience of the stage,' says Macready, 'has convinced me of the necessity of keeping, on the

day of exhibition, the mind as intent as possible on the subject of the actor's portraiture, even to the very moment of his entrance on the scene.' And again : ' Talma would dress some time before [the commencement of the performance] and make the peculiarities of his costume familiar to him ; at the same time that he thereby possessed himself more with the feeling of his character. I thought the practice so good, that I frequently adopted it, and derived great benefit from it.' Burbage, according to Fleckno, was 'a delightful Proteus, so wholly transforming himself into his parts, and putting off himself with his cloaths, as he never (not so much as in the tyring-house) assumed himself again until the play was done.' Anthony Aston tells us that ' *Betterton*, from the Time he was dress'd to the End of the Play, kept his Mind in the same Temperament and Adaptness, as the present Character required.' Salvini finds two or three hours of mental concentration an essential preliminary to entering with full conviction on such parts as Othello, Hamlet, or Saul ; and the ' transmigration,' as he calls it, once effected, endures unbroken throughout the play. Junius Brutus Booth who, in the maturity of his powers, was undoubtedly a magnificent actor, used to indulge in more than Salvini's two or three hours mental concentration. ' Whatever part he had to personate,' writes Mr. Edwin Booth (and that excellent tragedian evidently approves his father's practice), ' he was from the time of its rehearsal until he slept at night imbued with its very essence. If Othello was billed for the evening, . . . disregarding the fact

Talma, Reminiscences, i. p. 238

Burbage, Malone, iii. p. 185

Betterton, Aston, p. 5

Salvini

J. B. Booth, Matthews and Hutton, iii. p. 100

L

that Shakespeare's Moor was a Christian, he would mumble sentences from the Koran. . . . If Shylock was to be his part at night, he was a Jew all day ; and if in Baltimore at the time, he would pass hours with a learned Israelite, who lived near by, discussing Hebrew history!' The tendency to retain in the green-room the manner and voice of the character one is assuming appears to be common enough. ' I observed this tendency in Macready,' writes Mr. John Coleman, ' and Charles Kean had the same peculiarity in a less degree.' Mr. Kendal, too, used to notice this habit in Charles Kean and thought it an affectation. So it was, no doubt ; but the affectation may have arisen, not from vanity, but from deliberate artistic purpose. Mr. Kendal himself admits that between the acts of such a play as *The Ironmaster*, in which he leaves the stage and returns to it in high emotion, he would not willingly lapse into levity, because it would cost him unnecessary trouble to regain the right pitch of feeling. Many actors assure me that it is common for tragedians to shut themselves up in their dressing-rooms between the acts of a play, and to reassume their personage immediately on being called, sometimes even timing their walk from the dressing-room door to the wing, so as to be able to step upon the stage without a moment's pause. M. Albert Lambert writes :—' J'ai quelquefois conservé les allures et les grimaces typiques de quelques personnages, de ma loge au foyer, et du foyer à la scène. Par exemple pour Louis XI je conservais tant que je pouvais son

Macready and C. Kean

M. Lambert

sourire faux et sarcastique, son regard d'acier ; pour
Louis XIV son grand air impassible ; pour Alceste
son front rembruni et sa moue mécontente ; pour
Tartuffe sa marche glissante, son œil éteint, demi-
voilé, son sourire onctueux et son geste officiant ; pour
Harpagon sa grimace inquiète et nerveuse. Mais
seulement parce que ces masques sont historiques,
universels, et qu'il faut les apporter justes devant les
yeux du public.' Between Othello's exit and re-
entrance in the third act Mr. John Coleman would Mr. Coleman
always prowl up and down behind the scenes like a
wild animal, the stage being kept clear in order that
he might be safe from interruption. ' I always endea-
vour,' writes Mr. Wilson Barrett, ' to get a short time Mr. Wilson Barrett
to myself, in my dressing-room, to think over ·my
character and work myself into it, so to speak. It is
a trouble and annoyance to me to converse on any
subject while waiting to commence my work. I have
noticed the same thing in other actors.' Miss Wallis Miss Wallis
tells me that between the acts of a heavy part she
always retires to her dressing-room and maintains
absolute silence, not speaking even to her maid if
she can help it.

'Silence was the order my mother had given as Lady Martin, *Shake-speare's Female Characters*, p. 125
the rule for my dressing-room,' writes Lady Martin
—'no talk to take my thoughts from the work I had
in hand.' 'I was taken by my aunt early to the
theatre,' Fanny Kemble writes, 'and there in my Fanny Kemble, *Record of a Girlhood*, ii. p. 69
dressing-room sat through the entire play, when I
was not on the stage, with some piece of tapestry or
needlework, with which, during the intervals of my

tragic sorrows, I busied my fingers; my thoughts being occupied with the events of my next scene and the various effects it demanded.' Miss Wallis relates how she once visited Ristori in her dressing-room between the acts of *Maria Stuarda*, immediately after the scene between Mary and Elizabeth. The great actress received her, as it were, enthroned, and, though perfectly cordial, never once throughout the interview relaxed her queenly bearing. 'Affectation !' the reader may say; but again I add, affectation with an artistic purpose. 'Such an exaggeration,' Ristori writes to me, 'as identifying oneself all day with the character to be performed at night belongs to the conventions of the old school. My father, an experienced actor, who trained me for the stage, used to impress upon me that I should be melancholy for a whole day before playing a pathetic part—but I never acted up to his precepts. The true artist, indeed, before attacking an important part, will avoid all frivolous distractions ; but he need not meditate on mortality or weep like Heraclitus.' Let me mention in passing that Ristori, in her recently published Memoirs, professes herself so thorough an emotionalist

Etudes et Souvenirs, p. 85

that she never could 'feel' the passage where Mary Stuart pleads guilty to the murder of Darnley, because her historical studies had convinced her that this was a mistake on Schiller's part and that Mary was innocent !

These citations appear to me to prove conclusively that many distinguished actors have a difficulty in flinging themselves at one bound into the passion of a scene, and find it advantageous to keep themselves more or less completely in touch with their personage during the whole time of performance. On the other hand, there is no reason to doubt that some temperaments require less 'innervation,' to use Darwin's word, than others, or that, with a few, an infinitesimal space of time suffices. It is to be remembered, however, that if the keeping up of a character behind the scenes may be due to affectation, the total dropping of it may, in some cases, be no less affected. There is a motive (the avoidance of ridicule) for the latter affectation; none, except the artistic motive, for the former.

'Le véritable acteur,' says M. Coquelin, 'est toujours prêt. Il peut prendre son rôle à n'importe quel moment, et susciter immédiatement l'impression qu'il désire.' I think there is ample evidence that the veritable actor, in this sense, is a rare bird.

CHAPTER X.

THE BROWNIES OF THE BRAIN.

THE real paradox of acting, it seems to me, resolves itself into the paradox of dual consciousness. If it were true that the actor could not experience an emotion without absolutely yielding up his whole soul to it, then Diderot's doctrine, though still a little overstated, would be right in the main. But the mind is not so constituted. If the night of the murder of Duncan had been a fit time for psychological argument, Macduff might safely have moved an amendment to Macbeth's proposition :

Who can be wise, amazed, temperate and furious,
Loyal and neutral in a moment? No man.

There are many 'brownies,' as Mr. Stevenson puts it, in the actor's brain, and one of them may be agonising with Othello, while another is criticising his every tone and gesture, a third restraining him from strangling Iago in good earnest, and a fourth wondering whether the play will be over in time to let him catch his last train. I was anxious to obtain authentic illustrations of this double, triple, and quadruple action of the mind, and to that end framed the following question : —

Can you give any examples of the two or more strata of consciousness, or lines of thought, which must co-exist in your mind while acting? In other words, can you describe and illustrate how one part of your mind is given up to your character, while another part is criticising minutely your own gestures and intonations, and a third, perhaps, is watching the audience, or is busied with some pleasant or unpleasant recollection or anticipation in your private life?

It has been objected that the phrase 'must co-exist' begs the question; but is there really any question to beg? I looked upon the double action of the brain as a matter of universal experience, a thing to be assumed just as one assumes that the normal man has two legs. I did not regard it as a tendency peculiar to actors, but common to all men. It seemed to me, however, that acting must beget special forms of this multiple activity, and I hoped to obtain some clear and convincing illustrations of it.

Fanny Kemble's self-analysis deserves to rank as the classic passage on this point :—' The curious part of acting, to me, is the sort of double process which the mind carries on at once, the combined operation of one's faculties, so to speak, in diametrically opposite directions; for instance, in that very last scene of Mrs. Beverley, while I was half dead with crying in the midst of the *real* grief, created by an entirely *unreal* cause, I perceived that my tears were falling like rain all over my silk dress, and spoiling it; and I calculated and measured most accurately the space that my father would require to fall in, and moved myself and my train accordingly in the midst of the anguish I was to feign, and absolutely did endure.'

Fanny Kemble, Record of a Girlhood, ii. p. 103

It is this watchful faculty (perfectly prosaic and commonplace in its nature), which never deserts me while I am uttering all that exquisite passionate poetry in Juliet's balcony scene, while I feel as if my own soul was on my lips, and my colour comes and goes with the intensity of the sentiment I am expressing; which prevents me from falling over my train, from setting fire to myself with the lamps placed close to me, from leaning upon my canvas balcony when I seem to throw myself all but over it.'

No less interesting is Miss Clara Morris's account *Matthews and Hutton, v. p. 224* of her triple consciousness :—' There are, when I am on the stage,' she writes, 'three separate currents of thought in my mind; one in which I am keenly alive to Clara Morris, to all the details of the play, to the other actors and how they act, and to the audience ; another about the play and the character I represent ; and, finally, the thought that really gives me stimulus for acting. For instance, when I repeat such and such a line it fits like words to music to this underthought, which may be of some dead friend, of a story of Bret Harte's, of a poem, or may be even some pathetic scrap from a newspaper.' Miss Morris is here speaking of parts which from frequent repetition have lost their first effect upon *Post, p. 175* her. Her account of her method of working up emotion will be found on a later page.

M. Paul Mounet, Revue d'Art Dramatique, March 1, 1888 Another excellent witness to the same effect is Paul Mounet, of the Odéon, who has described to M. Larcher ' le dédoublement qui s'opère en lui quand il est en scène: il y a en lui *quelqu'un* qui le regarde et l'écoute : alors il joue véritablement de lui-même, comme un musicien joue de son instrument. Quelquefois l'artiste s'emporte : *l'autre* le voit, mais il se laisse griser délicieusement en sa compagnie. Ces jours-là, il dépasse la mesure et rentre mécontent dans la coulisse. Mais s'il est resté maître de lui, s'il s'est fait plaisir à lui-même, il est sûr de l'effet qu'il a produit : il a triomphé du public parce qu'il a triomphé de lui-même.' M. Mounet's comrade M. Albert Lambert writes :—' J'ai connu un artiste ne jouant qu'avec la sensibilité et une émotion que ne dominait pas toujours l'Art, s'apercevoir au plus fort d'une scène, que sa femme causait avec le pompier de service, s'en plaindre tout bas à son partner et continuer sa scène dans le même mouvement et dans la même émotion. J'ai quelquefois écouté " chanter mes effets," mais ceci c'est la corde raide, un seul faux pas et l'on glisse.' {.float-right}M. Lambert

There is an anecdote of Talma, after a scene of violent emotion, meeting his dresser at the wing and proceeding to abuse him roundly for not having polished his boots ; the implication being that he had noticed the man's remissness while at the height of his passion. An actor who once played Horatio to a very famous Hamlet tells me that in the last act he felt the shoulder of his cloak quite wet with the tragedian's tears at the line ' What ! the fair Ophelia,' yet that Hamlet's first remark on leaving the scene was, ' That damned organ was playing too loud all the time ! ' Such instances could be cited by the score. Indeed I have already quoted several of them {.float-right}Talma, *Lardin*

Ante, pp. 29, 71

in speaking of self-control, which is nothing but a manifestation of this dual consciousness.

Many actors—a surprising number, indeed—seem to be quite unaware of any double action of the mind. Some resent the suggestion, as though it implied carelessness or unconscientiousness on their part. Others simply reply that the actor should be 'absorbed' in his character, and seem powerless to analyse the state they describe as absorption. Others, again, relate curious incidents of the freaks of consciousness or of memory which occur in the course of long runs. Mr. Dion Boucicault, for example, states that when he has been playing a part for many months his mind is always occupied with other matters during the performance ; 'and this to such an extent that when, desiring for some special reason to act my best, I turn my thoughts upon my part, I forget the words, and, to recover them, feel obliged to think of something else.' Interesting as it is, this experience is not what I wanted to get at. Here the playing of the part has become quite automatic, leaving the mind free to occupy itself as best it may. The very complex movements of piano-playing have been known (says Dr. Carpenter) to become so purely automatic as to be performed in sleep ; and many pianists who know a piece of music thoroughly by heart will go wrong when they attempt to play with the notes before them. There is sometimes a difficulty, of course, in distinguishing between automatic action and the conscious or sub-conscious mental activity to which my question refers.

Mr. Bouci-cault

Here is a case in which this difficulty presents itself. 'Not long ago,' writes Miss Isabel Bateman, 'I had to give a recitation after the play, and, feeling rather anxious about it, I found myself repeating the poem (a long one) during the third act of the play. I went through the whole recitation while acting my part, not only repeating the words, but calling to mind the different effects I wished to produce. I confess this with a feeling of guilt, but I don't think anyone can have noticed a difference in my playing.' The question here is : Had Miss Bateman played her part so long as to have reached the automatic stage ? If not, this is a most curious instance of dual action. Mr. Leonard Outram informs me that, in playing James Ralston in the third act of *Jim the Penman*, where Mrs. Ralston cross-questions her husband as to the cause of his nervous excitement, he finds himself reading, with full comprehension, odds and ends from a newspaper which he happens to have in his hand. Here again one would like to know how often Mr. Outram has played the part ; but the passage is one of such complexity that it would certainly take a very long time to render the playing of it quite automatic.

'When working in earnest,' writes Mr. Forbes Robertson, 'I can only admit two strata, so to speak : one stratum, the part, the creature I am for the time ; the other, that part of my mind which circumstances and the surroundings compel me to give up to all things coming under the head of mechanical execution. I have experienced the other strata after a long run, and always fight against them, for I know they

Miss Isabel Bateman

Mr. L. Outram

Mr. Forbes Robertson

only mean that my work is getting mechanical.'
Even more to the point is the following reply from
Miss Janet Achurch : ' The only double line of
thought I like to have on the stage is a mental criticism on my own performance : " I got that exclamation
better than last night," or " I'm sure I'm playing this
scene slower than usual," and so on. I suppose no
one can help doing this ; but any thought that comes
to my mind outside my part I always stamp out as
quickly as possible.' This is precisely the form of
experience I wished to get at. Salvini, on the other
hand, declares that the careful self-criticism to which
he subjects himself is strictly confined to moments of
reflection after the performance is over. It may be
questioned whether this does not imply an under-
current of involuntary and unconscious self-criticism
running parallel with the action. The most miraculous memory will scarcely reproduce a cry or an
intonation so clearly as to allow of its effect being
estimated to a nicety. An instinctive sense of ap-
proval or disapproval must surely accompany its
actual utterances.

Some artists who profess themselves unconscious
of any double action of the mind unintentionally bear
witness to its existence. ' There is no better sponge
for one's tears,' says an actor of great pathetic power,
' than the sight of an overfed noodle asleep in the
stalls ' ; and a very distinguished actress confesses
to having ' played at ' a peculiarly stolid and stony
woman of fashion whom she observed among the
audience, determined to move her or perish in the

THE BROWNIES OF THE BRAIN   157

attempt. Here we have clearly an attitude of mind quite inconsistent with 'absorption' in the obvious sense of the word. Another leading actor mentions a curious circumstance which bears upon this point. If a momentary uneasiness causes him to make some slight gesture not essential to his part—for instance, if a twinge of neuralgia leads him to put his hand to his brow—he will often make the same gesture at the same point on the following night, without the recurrence of its cause: whereupon he immediately wonders why he did so, and recalls, by a distinct effort of thought, the sensation of the previous evening. In this case, what I have called the critical part of the actor's mind is evidently watching the executant part with great intentness. Another mode of consciousness which manifests itself in many actors may be called commercial rather than critical. 'I know people,' writes Mr. J. B. Howard, of Edinburgh, 'who, while on the stage, can count a well-filled house, and sum up the cash almost to a fraction.' This faculty seems to be not uncommon.

I am indebted to Miss Wallis for two most interesting illustrations of dual activity of mind. In a large provincial town, one day, she was advertised to appear as Juliet. A few hours before the time of the performance, her little daughter was taken suddenly and seriously ill. She sent to the theatre to say that she could not possibly appear ; but, the doctor assuring her that the child was in no immediate danger, she eventually determined not to disappoint the public. Never, she says, did she enter more

Miss Wallis

thoroughly into the part, and never did she play it with greater effect. She was strung up by excitement to a higher emotional pitch than she could ordinarily attain. And all the time the best part of her mind was with her child. Messengers were passing to and fro all the evening between her hotel and the theatre, and the bulletins, fortunately, were reassuring. She came out of the ordeal exhausted in body and mind, and would naturally be very loth to go through it again. Such an experience proves that two modes of intense activity may co-exist in the mind, each being, no doubt, resolvable into several subdivisions, if the memory could but reproduce them with sufficient distinctness. In the second case related by Miss Wallis a purely intellectual process of some complexity accompanied the performance of an exacting emotional scene. She was playing the title-part in Mr. Wills's *Ninon* at the Crystal Palace, where she had never appeared before. The moment she uttered her first speech she was conscious of a distracting echo in the theatre. She felt that if it were to continue she could scarcely get through her part, and she set to work to discover the right pitch of voice for this oddly-constructed building. She was somewhat consoled, before long, to find that the audience seemed unconscious of the reverberation, but she noticed that her fellow-actors were quite bewildered by it. Observing closely the effects produced by her comrades, and experimenting with her own voice, she at last hit on the right pitch, but not until the first act was nearly over. We have here a complex process of observa-

tion and reasoning running parallel with the playing
of an arduous emotional scene. I should add that
this was Miss Wallis's first appearance on the stage
after a long period of rest, so that her performance of
Ninon, so far from being automatic, must have involved
a considerable effort of memory and attention. 'And
a vivid emotional process,' Miss Wallis herself would
add ; but it is not essential to this part of my argument to determine whether the executant mode of
mental activity, in any particular instance, is or is not
informed by emotion.

This may be the fittest place to point out that the
double or treble strata of consciousness afford a simple
solution of one of the favourite anti-emotionalist
difficulties. If the tragedian felt with Orestes or
Œdipus, cries Diderot, 'his lot would be the most
wretched on earth.' That he should feel with them
as much as the spectator feels with them would
clearly not involve a chronic state of 'wretchedness';
for the fact that we take positive pleasure in the
most poignant imaginary woes, though a paradox, is
also a commonplace. It is the foundation and justi-
fication of tragedy. But it is quite possible that the
tragedian should habitually feel with his character
far more vividly than the average spectator—that he
should feel to the extent of actual unmetaphoric suffering—and yet should not be 'the most wretched'
of men. Severe suffering on one mental plane is
quite consistent with perfect contentment, nay, with
absolute beatitude, on another. Happiness and misery
reside in the deeps of consciousness ; the upper strata

Ante, p. 25

are of small account. I have a three months' holi-
day ; I put money in my purse and take passage for
Naples in an Orient steamer. We encounter a capful
of wind in the Bay of Biscay, and I am prostrated by
seasickness for fifty or sixty hours.   I probably suffer
more agony than consumption or cancer could inflict
in a similar space of time ; yet I am not really miserable ; my fundamental consciousness is one of de-
lighted anticipation ; for

> I shall see, before I die,
> The palms and temples of the South.

Conversely, the maxim 'Let us eat and drink, for
to-morrow we die' is the veriest mockery unless we
put a liberal interpretation on 'to-morrow.' Treat it
prosaically—place our death-warrant in our napkin—
and a banquet fit for Lucullus will have small savour
in our nostrils. So may it be with the actor. The
surface of his consciousness may be tormented and
tempest-tossed while the depths are unruffled. It
may even be that the more really and acutely he
suffers—the more thoroughly he merges himself in
his part—the greater may be his fundamental happiness ; for he knows that he is triumphing, and
his spirit is glad. I am far from arguing that
mimetic woes ever attain, or ought to attain, the
full poignancy of the real miseries they represent.
All I wish to point out is that actors may quite
well undergo states of feeling which may fairly be described as suffering—genuine and acute suffering—
without being on that account the most miserable
of men.

Another section of my interrogatory was designed to throw further light on this question of double consciousness, especially with reference to Diderot's assumption that to 'feel' a part implies absolute and, so to speak, helpless absorption in it.

> Diderot tells how Lekain, in a scene of violent emotion, saw an actress's diamond earring lying on the stage, and had presence of mind enough to kick it to the wing instead of treading on it. Can you relate any similar instances of presence of mind? And should you regard them as showing that the actor is personally unmoved by the situation in which he is figuring?

Lekain
Ante, p. 29

The anecdote of Lekain is regarded by the anti-emotionalists as a tower of strength; but its foundations are sadly insecure. Not that there is any reason to doubt the fact. On the contrary, similar incidents have come within the experience of every artist. It is the interpretation that is more than doubtful. Intense emotion, as I have already suggested, will often act upon the mind, not as chloroform but rather as curari. It places all the faculties on the alert, and stimulates every function of mind and body. The apathy of mere dejection may beget that relaxation of the nerves which places us at the mercy of trifling accidents; the excitement of violent feeling has rather the opposite effect. So far as the incident of the diamond is concerned, Lekain might even have been labouring under the whole emotion of the real Ninias; much more may he have been experiencing the similar though less poignant emotional state— the agony *con sordino*—begotten by the imagination.

Ante, p. 30

M

A few of the artists whom I have consulted—I may mention Mr. and Mrs. Bancroft, Mr. and Mrs. Kendal, and Mr. Clayton—hold that in certain crises of extreme emotional exaltation, an actor would be incapable of such presence of mind as that of Lekain. This, however, is a theoretical opinion rather than a statement founded on positive experience. I am informed of a score of instances in which jewels—even stage-jewels—have been adroitly rescued, but no one has related a single case in which the merest trinket has been sacrificed to the passion of the scene. My informants, moreover, are almost unanimous in holding that presence of mind in face of trifling misadventures by no means proves that the actor is personally unmoved. 'In a like case,' Mr. Forbes Robertson very aptly remarks, 'the second stratum of my mind would act for me without interfering with the first.' Mr. Beerbohm Tree takes precisely the view of the diamond anecdote which I have suggested above. He holds that Lekain's action may be just as rationally explained on the hypothesis of extreme emotional tension as on that of perfect placidity. Mr. Tree tells of an analogous case within his own experience, in which a young actress, of highly emotional temperament, exhibited even greater presence of mind. She was grovelling at the feet of a stony-hearted inquisitor, praying desperately for the life of someone dear to her, when a diamond fell from her hair. She noted where it lay, put her left hand to her brow for a moment, and then let it fall, as though in the lassitude of despair, precisely upon the stray

Mr. Forbes Robertson

Mr. Beerbohm Tree

jewel. The gesture was so appropriate that the audience suspected nothing, and the effect of the passage was, if anything, heightened. Yet there is not the smallest reason to suppose that this lady— a convinced emotionalist—was, on this occasion only, simulating in cold blood the violent emotion of the scene.

Salvini tells me that on one occasion, while play- *Salvini* ing Orosmane in *Zaïre*, he suddenly felt, in the middle of the fourth act, that the belt which sustained his Turkish trousers had given way. Horror of horrors! What was to be done? As if in an access of passion, he dashed at a tiger-skin which covered the divan and swathed it round his body. The public 'non fece motto,' and in this improvised kilt he finished the act. 'I was told,' he says, 'that I had never played the scene with greater intensity of rage, irony and despair.' 'I never lose my presence of mind,' writes Miss Bateman (Mrs. Crowe). 'I was *Miss* once acting with a gentleman who played my lover, *Bateman* and in his death agonies his wig came off. Luckily I wore a long mantle, and was able to hide the mishap by throwing a corner of it over the gentleman's head. Dozens of such accidents have happened to me, and I don't remember once failing to meet the emergency.' An extreme case of adroitness under difficulties is related by an actor of great experience. He was playing the very stormy love-scene in *Peril*, which ends in the lover chasing the unwilling fair one round and round the room. The lady wore a girdle of large and costly artificial pearls, and, just as this culminating point was reached, the string broke, scattering the pearls all over the stage. 'We finished the scene,' writes my informant, ' without any hesitation or any change of business, and neither of us crushed a single pearl. This shows that we had not lost our senses—that's all.'   I should add that the hero of this dramatic egg-dance is, on the whole, an anti-emotionalist ; but the incident is none the less a striking example of dual activity of mind.

Historical instances of presence of mind are simply innumerable. Baron, in *Le Comte d'Essex*, noticing in the course of his scene with Cecil that his garter had come unfastened, heightened the effect of contempt at which he was aiming by coolly stooping to tie it without pausing in his speech. Brizard, a great tragedian of last century, was playing an heroic part when the plumes of his casque caught fire. He remained unconscious of the accident until the audience called his attention to it, when, without interrupting his declamation, he calmly took off the burning headpiece and handed it to his confidant. What the confidant did, history saith not. Such anecdotes as these meet us at every turn, but as they seem to me to afford no evidence, one way or another, as to the actor's emotional state, I do not think them worth collecting. More to the point, perhaps, are the common anecdotes of actors interpolating personal asides to their fellow-performers in scenes of high emotion. Diderot gives an elaborate instance of this in the shape of a conjugal quarrel between an actor and actress, carried on under cover of a scene between Eraste and

Baron,
Lemazurier, i. p. 95

Brizard,
Lemazurier, i. p. 173

Pollock, p. 32

Lucile in *Le Dépit Amoureux.* How Diderot should be in a position to report their asides he does not explain, and in the absence of such explanation we cannot help suspecting the episode to be imaginary. But supposing it genuine, and supposing (a difficult admission) that Molière's dialogue was as effectively delivered as Diderot represents it to have been, we must still remember that the scene is not one which could in any case make great claims upon the emotions of the performers. More credible and more to the purpose is an anecdote of Garrick, which I find in the *Monthly Mirror* for 1807. 'A medical gentleman of eminence,' it appears, once remarked to 'Tom King the comedian,' that Garrick must have suffered greatly from 'the exertion of his feelings.' 'Pooh!' replied the original Sir Peter Teazle, ' he suffer from his feelings! Why, Sir, I was playing with him one night in *Lear*, when, in the middle of a most passionate and afflicting part, and when the whole house was drowned in tears, he turned his head round to me, and putting his tongue in his cheek, whispered '*Damme, Tom, it'll do!* So much for stage feeling.' A precisely similar story is told of Edmund Kean when playing Brutus to the Titus of his son Charles in Howard Payne's tragedy of *Brutus*. 'The strong interest of the play,' says Charles Kean's biographer, ' combined with the natural acting of father and son, completely subdued the audience. They sat suffused in tears during the last pathetic interview, until Brutus, overpowered by his emotions, falls on the neck of Titus, exclaiming in a burst of agony, "Embrace thy wretched father";

New Series, i. p. 78
Garrick

Edmund Kean

Cole, i. p. 163

when they broke forth into the relief of loud and
prolonged peals of approbation. Edmund Kean then
whispered in his son's ear, " Charley, we are doing
· the trick." ' These anecdotes are so exactly alike as to
arouse a suspicion that the second may be nothing but
the first revamped, according to a principle familiar to
students of (theatrical) comparative mythology. The
incidents themselves, however, are so probable that
both may quite well be genuine. But do they prove
that Garrick and Kean were unmoved ? Surely not.
The executant section or stratum of their minds may
have been wrung with emotion, while the observant
section, conscious of the success thus attained, found
a safety-valve for its excitement in a hurried whisper

John
Mason.
*Record of a
Girlhood,
ii. p.* 28

of self-congratulation.   ' My cousin, John Mason,'
writes Fanny Kemble, ' the first time he acted Romeo
with me, though a very powerful muscular young man,
whispered to me as he carried my corpse down the
stage with a fine semblance of frenzy, " Jove, Fanny,
you are a lift ! " ' There is a clear distinction between this playful whisper and the exultant asides of
Garrick and Kean. Mr. Mason, in all probability,
was really unmoved, and therefore, according to
Diderot, possessed the first qualification for a ' sublime ' actor. How many of my readers, I wonder,
have so much as heard his name ?

Ant:, p. 31

The anti-emotionalists, as I have remarked before,
should let presence of mind alone, and rather adduce
instances of the evil effects of that absence of mind
which they hold to be one of the manifestations of
' sensibility.' Unfortunately for their argument, the

total absorption in one mode of feeling which numbs
the intellect and deadens the sense is of very rare
occurrence in real life, and still rarer, of course, on the
stage. If this were not so, we should hear every
day of some mediocre Othello strangling his Iago,
or some second-rate Juliet stabbing herself in sad
earnest. The classical case in point is the manslaughter
(or slave-slaughter) committed by the Roman actor
Æsopus, as set forth by Plutarch in his *Life of*
Cicero :—' Yet it is reported notwithstanding, that for
his [Cicero's] gesture and pronunciation, having the
selfesame defects of nature at the beginning, which
Demosthenes had, to reforme them, he carefully studied
to counterfeit *Roscius*, an excellent Comedian, and
Æsope also a player of Tragedies. Of this *Æsope* men
write, that he playing one day *Atreus* part upon a
stage (who determined with himselfe how he might be
revenged on his brother *Thyestes*) a servant by chance
having occasion to runne suddenly by him, he forget-
ting himselfe, striving to shew the vehement passion
and furie of this king, gave him such a blow on his
head with the scepter in his hand, that he slue him
dead in the place.' François Riccoboni's comment on
this incident is conceived in such a nobly antique spirit
that I cannot forbear quoting it :—' Pourquoi ne tua-t-
il jamais,' he asks, ' aucun des Comédiens qui jouoient
avec lui ? C'est que la vie d'un Esclave n'étoit rien,
mais qu'il étoit obligé de respecter celle d'un Citoyen.
Sa fureur n'étoit donc pas si vraye, puisqu'elle laissoit
à sa raison toute la liberté du choix. Mais en
Comédien habile il saisit l'occasion que le hasard lui

*Æsopus,
North's
transla-
tion, ed.
1631, p. 861*

*L'Art du
Théâtre,
p.* 40

présentoit.' There is no paltry humanitarianism about Riccoboni. Like many another actor, he doubtless deplored the pettifogging laws which forbid the occasional slaying of a 'super' when the situation demands, or the ' super ' deserves, his quietus. The affair (to speak seriously) was doubtless a pure accident, like many other ' true tragedies ' in the annals of the stage ; or else it was a case of temporary insanity.

Pollock, p. 107

Diderot, as in duty bound, declares Æsopus to have been but a middling actor. Two generations of Romans thought otherwise ; but their judgment was no doubt biassed by the fact that they had seen him.

Instances of helpless, somnambulistic absorption, such as would lead an actor to trample a valuable jewel under foot, are scarcely to be found. Two famous tragedians of the early French stage, Mondory

Mondory and Mont-fleury

and Montfleury, are both said to have died of their reckless self-abandonment to violent passion—the former out-Heroding Herod in *La Marianne* by Tristan l'Hermite, the latter playing Oreste in the original

Lemazurier, i. pp. 422, 426, 126

production of Racine's *Andromaque*. Both anecdotes, however, seem to be entirely apocryphal. Less doubtful is a fine instance of non-absorption afforded

Beaubourg

by the stately and stilted Beaubourg. In the character of Horace, he was pursuing Mlle. Duclos, as Camille, with sword upraised to kill her. In her haste to escape she tripped and fell ; whereupon Beaubourg politely took off his helmet with one hand, helped her with the other to rise, and handed her gallantly off the stage, as a preliminary to assassinating her behind the scenes. Holman, according to Reynolds, once gave himself up so rashly to the torrent, tempest, and whirlwind of his passion, that he missed his footing and fell headlong over the footlights into the midst of the astonished fiddlers. This catastrophe, however, was due to the unusual slope of a very small country stage. Mrs. Siddons, speaking to Reynolds, said, 'My brother John, in his most impetuous bursts, is always careful to avoid any discomposure of his dress or deportment; but in the whirlwind of passion, I lose all thought of such matters'; and Boaden says quaintly, 'When Mrs. Siddons quitted her dressing-room, I believe she left there the last thought about herself. Never did I see her eye wander from the business of the scene— no recognisance of the most noble of her friends exchanged the character for the individual.' Rachel, like John Kemble, remained perfectly conscious of every fold in her robe ; yet Fanny Kemble assures us that ' her wonderful fainting exclamation of " O, mon cher Curiace ! " lost none of its poignant pathos ' on that account. ' Criticising a portrait of herself in that scene, she said to the painter, " Ma robe ne fait pas ce pli-là ; elle fait, au contraire, celui-ci." The artist, inclined to defend his picture, asked her how, while she was lying with her eyes shut and feigning utter insensibility, she could possibly tell anything about the plaits of her dress. " Allez-y voir," replied Rachel ; and the next time she played Camille, the artist was able to convince himself by more careful observation that she was right.'

Holman, Reynolds, ii. p. 76

Kemble and Mrs. Siddons, Macready, i. p. 149

Boaden, ii. p. 289

Rachel

Record of a Girlhood, ii. p. 12

*Miss
O'Neill,
Macready
as I knew
him, p.* 29

*Lady
Martin,
Shake-
speare's
Female
Charac-
ters, p.* 115

On the other hand, I shall quote in the next chapter an extraordinary instance of absorption in a part which Fanny Kemble relates from her own experience. 'Miss O'Neill,' said Macready to Lady Pollock, 'was a remarkable instance of self-abandonment in acting. She forgot everything for the time but her assumed character. She was an entirely modest woman ; yet in acting with her I have been nearly smothered with her kisses.' From the time of Æsopus downwards, however, I can find only one authentic instance of absorption carried to a dangerous pitch. It is recorded in Lady Martin's delightful series of autobiographical criticisms. Describing her first performance of Juliet, she writes :—' When the time came to drink the potion, there was none ; for the phial had been crushed in my hand, the fragments of glass were eating their way into the tender palm, and the blood was trickling down in a little stream over my pretty dress. This had been for some time apparent to the audience, but the Juliet knew nothing of it, and felt nothing, until the red stream arrested her attention. . . . This never occurred again, because they ever afterwards gave me a wooden phial.' On this occasion Miss Faucit would no doubt have trampled on the Koh-i-noor had it lain in her path ; but then she was a child of thirteen, and it was her first appearance on any stage.

Before leaving this branch of my subject, let me illustrate by three anecdotes three different degrees of dramatic absorption. The first (related by Mr. John Coleman, who was present on the occasion) goes to show that some artists are apt on occasion to yield themselves up with painful completeness to the illusion of the scene. Mr. and Mrs. Charles Kean were one night playing *The Gamester* at Belfast. . It was their benefit ; the house was crowded, and the play went electrically. It closes with a piece of 'business' said to have been invented by Mrs. Siddons. After the death of Beverley, Jarvis and Charlotte attempt to lead Mrs. Beverley away ; but she turns at the door, and, as the curtain falls, flings herself in an agony of grief upon the body of her husband. On this parti-cular evening Mrs. Kean had become so absorbed in her part that she could not shake off the illusion even when the play was over, and astonished the bystanders by vehemently shaking her husband as he lay on his pallet-bed, and crying piteously, ' Oh, my Charley !— my poor darling—you are not dead ; say you are not dead !' 'Deuce a bit, my darling !' responded Kean. ' But tell me so—tell me so, Charley !' ' I *am* telling you so, Nelly ; but there, there—come and get dressed for Violante.' 'Good gracious !' exclaimed Mrs. Kean, immediately recovering herself, ' it's wonderful I should have forgot about *The Wonder* ; Servant, ladies and gentlemen !' And so, with a stately curt-sey, she made her way to her dressing-room.

My second illustration is more ambiguous. In the fifth act of *Othello*, while Emilia is knocking at the door, and the Moor, in anguish of soul, is half rueing the deed he has but half done, a celebrated tragedian is in the habit of seizing a moment, when he is concealed from the audience by the curtain of

Mrs. C. Kean

Desdemona's bed, to drink a glass of water held in
readiness for him by his servant! In some actors
such a device might fairly be taken as a sign of callousness. The particular artist in question, however, is
an uncompromising emotionalist in theory, and, as I
have ample grounds for believing, in practice as well.
The just conclusion to be drawn, it seems to me, is that
the accomplished artist, even in the very tempest and
whirlwind of passion, retains sufficient self-mastery to
neglect no means of economising or reinforcing his
physical resources.

The third anecdote takes us to the opposite end
of the scale, illustrating that sublime perfection of
self-command which belongs to the actor of Diderot's
ideal. Some years ago an old playgoer went to see a
popular drama in which a very popular actor played
an heroic part. He noticed that the popular actor not
only shouted very loud, but kept on changing his key
in an eccentric fashion. Shortly afterwards he met
one of the supernumeraries, whom he happened to
know, and they fell to discussing the play. 'What
did you think of Mr. So-and-So?' asked the super.
'Magnificent!' replied the old playgoer, diplomatic-
ally; 'but why does he shout in such different keys?'
'Oh, don't you know the reason of that, sir?' answered
the super. 'That's to keep the men up to their work.
When he changes his key it's to show that the lime-
light isn't on him!' If the *Paradoxe* were anything
more than a paradox, this actor should be among the
greatest of his age.

CHAPTER XI.

'DAMNABLE ITERATION.'

A NECESSARY corollary to the anti-emotionalist theory—and Diderot was not the man to shrink from it—is that long runs, far from being the bane of art, must be its salvation. He speaks with admiration of a Neapolitan company which was drilled until the actors were ' épuisés de la fatigue de ces répétitions multipliées, ce que nous appelons blasés,' and then performed for six months on end, ' while the Sovereign and his subjects enjoyed the highest pleasure that can be obtained from stage-illusion.' Since Diderot had thus committed himself, I was forced to put the following question, though the subject has been so often thrashed out of late that I could not hope to elicit any very novel or interesting evidence :—

Pollock, p. 82

> With reference to long runs : does frequent repetition induce callousness to the emotions of a part? Do you continue to improve during a certain number of representations and then remain stationary, or deteriorate? Or do you go on elaborating a part throughout a long run ? Or do you improve in some respects and deteriorate in others ?

The general tenor of the answers was a foregone conclusion. My informants are almost unanimous in holding the long-run system noxious. Some suffer more than others from the frequent repetition of a part ; some are more alive than others to the element of novelty afforded by the changing audiences ; some have a greater tendency than others to keep on working at and developing a part, studying new refinements and attempting improved effects ; but all agree that there is a limit even to these alleviations of the evil, and that ultimately they either deteriorate or have to make a painful effort to keep up to the mark. No one who has ever seen a play after its fiftieth consecutive night will have any doubt on this point. Some artists, indeed, assert that the emotional passages of a part never grow stale to them, though they admit that in lighter scenes their playing suffers.

Miss Bateman Miss Ward
'If I really feel a part,' writes Miss Bateman, ' I never get tired of it.' Miss Geneviève Ward believes in the possibility of improvement throughout a long run, but admits that after playing *Forget-me-not* more than 500 times, she 'passed through a period of apathy, lasting several months.' One or two other artists add qualifying circumstances to their condemnation of long runs, but no one seriously defends them.

The truth is that Diderot had no means of studying long runs and their effect. He cites from hearsay the Neapolitan practice, but he probably never saw a piece which had been played, by the same players, more than a score or so of times, and these not consecutive, but spread over months or years. Had he seen *La Tosca* on its 99th night or *Our Boys* on its

999th night, he would probably have suppressed the passage as to 'the highest pleasure that can be obtained from stage-illusion.' The true anti-emotionalist position as to long runs should be, not that they are positively beneficial, but that an actor who is an automaton from the first suffers less than one who begins by playing from the heart and gradually hardens into automatism. At the same time (as we have already seen in the case of laughter), it is easy to overrate the tendency of mere repetition to deaden the sensibilities. An inordinate number of *consecutive* repetitions is necessarily mischievous. ' In order to obtain the right mood,' says Miss Clara Morris, 'after the part has become so familiar that the woes of the personage cease to affect me, I am obliged to resort to outside influence ; that is, I indulge in the luxury of grief by thinking over somebody else's woes, and when everything else fails, I think that I am dead and then I cry for myself !' No one can go through the same series of emotions six times in a week (or seven or eight times in the case of matinées) for a series of months or years without becoming jaded. But with proper intervals of rest and change, a great artist (of this there is plentiful proof) can enter into the emotions of Othello and Juliet even unto seventy times seven. ' After feeling a part intensely on one night,' says Miss Wallis, 'the reaction makes it impossible to enter into it thoroughly on the following evening. Therefore an alternation of parts, and especially of such parts as Juliet and Rosalind— tragedy and comedy— is a blessed, and even essential,

Ante, p. 113

Matthews and Hutton, v. p. 224

Miss Wallis

Lady
Martin,
*Shake-
speare's
Female
Charac-
ters, p.* 181

relief.' The system of every well-regulated theatre, in every country save England and America, provides for the necessary rest and change, and it is only of late years in our own country that the ' 500th consecutive performance' has become the one goal of managerial ambition. 'Repetition, certainly, had no effect,' writes Lady Martin, 'in making the [potion-] scene less vivid to my imagination. The last time I played Juliet, which was in Manchester in 1871, I fainted on the bed at the end of it, so much was I overcome with the reality of the " thick-coming fancies." ' But then Lady Martin had never played Juliet five hundred, or even fifty, times in succession. Nor has Salvini worn his Othello threadbare in this reckless fashion.

CHAPTER XII.

THE SPUR OF THE MOMENT.

IT is generally assumed that the actor who, by nature or training, is superior to the foibles of sensibility, will have every smallest detail of his playing regulated in advance, even to the motion of a finger or the raising of an eyebrow. On the other hand, a tendency to rely on momentary impulse is one of the protean forms of sensibility discussed in the *Paradoxe*. Therefore I formulated the following questions :—

Do you ever yield to sudden inspirations of accent or gesture occurring in the moment of performance ? And are you able to note, and subsequently reproduce, such inspirations ? Have you ever produced a happy effect by pure chance or by mistake, and then incorporated it permanently in your performance ?

In my chapter on the *Paradoxe* I have discussed the limitations placed upon momentary impulse by the fact that the actor is part of a complex mechanism which would be brought to a standstill by any great irregularity in the action of one of its wheels. These limits are wide enough, however, to admit of very important variations, and it is interesting to study the practice of different artists in admitting or excluding the suggestions of the moment.

Ante, p. 24

N

In an 'Introductory Discourse' to the second
English edition of Luigi Riccoboni's *General History
of the Stage* we find some curious details as to the
methods of the great actors of last century. The
writer is anonymous, but the date, the style, and the
fact of his anonymity suggest that he may have been
none other than the author of *The Actor*. He emphatically recommends the English actors of his time
to imitate the variety of the Italians. 'With us,' he
says, 'the same Scene is always played in the same
Manner, not only by the same Actor, but by every
Actor who performs it : We know, therefore, before it
comes, all that we are to admire. Perhaps there never
was a greater or a juster Piece of Action upon the
Theatre of any Country, than that consummate Player
Mr. *Barry* threw into his character of the Earl of
Essex, when his Wife fell into a Swoon, and he was
going to Execution ; but 'twas every Night the same.
In this Manner al;o that beautiful, though perhaps
not proper, Attitude of *Romeo* at the Tomb, is always
the same, not only in Mr. *Barry* and in Mr. *Garrick*,
every Time each plays, but 'tis the same in both.
[This probably refers to Romeo's then traditional
gesture of threatening Paris with the crowbar.] On
the contrary, let an *Italian* please ever so greatly once
in his Scene, he never courts a second Applause by
the same Attitude . . . these People having that true
Enthusiasm to conceive themselves really the Persons
they represent. . . . In the Tragedy of *Boadicea*,
which but for this cloying Repetition would certainly
have pleased more than nine Nights, we had an

London,
1754, *pp.*
xiv–xx

Barry

Garrick

The Actor,
(1755) *p.*
283

Instance of the Fault in the greatest player in the World. . . . Mr. *Garrick*, in the character of *Dumnorix* in this Play, drew his Sword on the first Night in the midst of a Prayer ; and full of the Uprightness of his Cause, brandished it in the Face of Heaven : It was disputed whether this were proper ; but there could be no Dispute whether a Repetition of it could be proper ; that was impossible. The Suddenness of a virtuous Emotion might excuse him once in doing it ; but nothing could justify the cold Repetition.' Mrs. Cibber and Mrs. Pritchard this critic praises for their variety—also, ' that new Actress named before, who, tho' always the same haughty, jealous, fond *Hermione*, never was twice indebted to the same Set of Attitudes and Gestures to express that Excellence.' This ' new actress' I take to have been a Mrs. Gregory.

Davies, on the other hand, asserts that Garrick, ' of all players he ever knew, gave the greatest variety to action and deportment ' ; citing as an unaccountable exception to this rule the constant uniformity of his action at the close of the Play Scene in *Hamlet*. At the lines

> For some must watch, while some must sleep :
> Thus runs the world away,

' it was his constant practice to pull out a white handkerchief, and, walking about the stage, to twirl it round with vehemence.' It is said (though I can cite no good authority) that he always gave the handkerchief three twirls, and that it was once noted as an innovation that he twirled it a fourth time. His personal theory, given under his own hand and seal, not

Side notes: Mrs. Cibber and Mrs. Pritchard

Garrick, *Dramatic Miscellanies, iii. p. 96*

N 2

Mlle.
Clairon,
*Garrick's
Correspon-
dence, i.
p.* 359

only left room for, but insisted on, the inspiration of the moment. 'What shall I say to you, my dear friend, about the "Clairon"?' he writes to Sturz in 1769. 'Your dissection of her is as accurate as if you had opened her alive ; she has everything that art and a good understanding, with great natural spirit, can give her. But then I fear (and I only tell you my fears and open my soul to you) the heart has none of those instantaneous feelings, that life-blood, that keen sensibility, that bursts at once from genius, and, like electrical fire, shoots through the veins, marrow, bones and all, of every spectator. Madame Clairon is so conscious and certain of what she can do, that she never, I believe, had the feelings of the instant come upon her unexpectedly ; but I pronounce that the greatest strokes of genius have been unknown to the actor himself, till circumstances, and the warmth of the scene, has sprung the mine as it were, as much to his own surprise, as that of the audience. Thus I make a great difference between a great genius and a good actor. The first will always realise the feelings of his character, and be transported beyond himself ; while the other, with great powers, and good sense, will give great pleasure to an audience, but never

*Horace,
Epist. ii.*
1, 211

Pectus inaniter angit,
Irritat, mulcet, falsis terroribus implet
Ut magus.

I have with great freedom communicated my ideas of acting, but you must not betray me, my good friend ; the Clairon would never forgive me, though I called

her an excellent actress, if I did not swear by all the
Gods she was the greatest genius too.'

That this passage expresses Gárrick's deliberate
and enduring opinion, I am led to believe by a piece
of evidence whose value the reader must estimatè
for himself. In the British Museum Library there is
a copy of D'Hannetaire's *Observations sur l'Art du
Comédien* bearing the book-plate of ' T. Jolley, Esq.,
F.S.A.' On its title-page is written, doubtless in
Mr. Jolley's hand, the words ' *Garrick's copy* ' ; and I
find that Mr. Jolley bought it for two shillings at the
sale of Garrick's library in 1823. In discussing the
question of inspiration, D'Hannetaire observes :—
' Un bon maître, loin de jamais diversifier la manière
de rendre les différens morceaux d'une Tragédie ou
d'une Comédie, les débitera toujours invariablement
de même, au bout de dix ans, comme au bout de deux
heures.' Opposite this passage, in the margin, the
word ' *wrong* ' is faintly pencilled ; and four pages
further on, where D'Hannetaire remarks, ' qu'il n'est
qu'une manière de bien dire, de bien réciter,' the same
annotator interjects ' *wrong again.*' There is only one
other marginal note in the book : where the author
describes a dogmatic theorist on acting, the same hand
has pencilled ' [*M*]*acklin's* [*Ch*]*aracter*,' the bracketed
letters having been cut away in binding. Now, I
have very little doubt that these are Garrick's annotations. Making allowance for the difference between
a fine pen and a blunt pencil, I think the handwriting
greatly resembles his. The antecedent probabilities,
too, seem to me very strong. No one but an actor

Garrick

Paris, 1776

p. 45

p. 49

p. 70

would be likely to contradict D'Hannetaire on such a seemingly trifling point of theory; and we know from the letter to Sturz quoted above, that in 1769 Garrick held the opinion which (if I am right in my assumption) we now find him reiterating some time between 1776 and his death in 1779. The pencilled notes are certainly not in the same writing as '*Garrick's copy*' on the fly-leaf; and there is every reason to suppose, I think, that the book passed from Mr. Jolley's library to the Museum, without coming into other hands. The fact that part of one of the notes was cut off in binding before Mr. Jolley's book-plate was affixed to the cover, excludes the supposition that any reader at the Museum (in defiance of the regulations) can have recorded his private sentiments on the national property. The matter is of no great importance, for an opinion so deliberately expressed as that in the letter to Sturz can scarcely have been the whim of a moment. Yet, if I am right in my conjecture, Garrick's emphatic contradiction of two remarks and two only in D'Hannetaire's 487 pages of theory, proves that the artistic value of spontaneity was habitually and vividly present to his mind.

Clairon and Dumesnil   The criticism of Clairon in the letter to Sturz raises the question : Which of the rival queens of the French stage did Garrick most admire ? the frigid, measured, automatic Clairon, or the fiery, spontaneous, dæmonic Dumesnil ? These two actresses are held up by Diderot as types of what a great artist ought and *Pollock, pp. 9–12* ought not to be. 'Quel jeu plus parfait que celui de la Clairon ?' he asks. '. . . Elle sait par cœur tous les détails de son jeu comme tous les mots de son rôle. . . . Il n'en est pas de la Dumesnil ainsi que de la Clairon. Elle monte sur les planches sans savoir ce qu'elle dira ; la moitié du temps, elle ne sait ce qu'elle dit ; mais il vient un moment sublime.' Upon this passage Talma remarks, ' J'avoue que je préfère le jeu sublime au jeu parfait.' It was Dumesnil who, at the height of her frenzy in the part of Cléopatre, made the whole parterre (a standing pit no doubt) recoil several paces 'par un mouvement d'horreur, aussi vif que spontané.' It was she, too, who first dared to run on the French tragic scene. Playing the part of a mother whose son is threatened with death, she actually ran across the stage to ward off the fatal blow. Until then, says Lemazurier, ' on marchait plus ou moins vite sur le théâtre ; mais personne ne croyait possible d'y courir.' The effect was probably unrehearsed, and it took the audience by storm. Now, which of these great actresses did Garrick prefer ? ' Dumesnil,' says Boaden in his life of Mrs. Siddons, ' was the *explosive* heroine, the Clairon the profound calculator of all her effects '; and he adds that Garrick gave the palm to Clairon. Lemazurier, on the other hand, declares positively that Dumesnil was his favourite and that he said of Clairon, ' Elle est trop actrice.' Lemazurier does not state his authority, but the remark accords so exactly with the whole tone of the letter to Sturz that we can have little hesitation in accepting it as genuine. Fanny Kemble, too, states that Garrick described Clairon as the greatest *actress* of her age, but said of Dumesnil

Réflexions sur Lekain, p. 43

Lemazurier, ii. p. 195

Lemazurier, ii. p. 200

i. p. 219

Lemazurier, ii. p. 106

Record of a
Girlhood,
iii. p. 91
that in her he forgot the actress and saw only Phèdre,
Rodogune and Hermione. She does not give her
authority for this statement, which may very likely
have been a tradition in her family. Voltaire, according to Lemazurier, was also at heart of the Dumesnil
Lema-
zurier, ii.
p. 200
faction :—' Il ne balança jamais à lui accorder la pré-
férence qu'elle méritait, et s'il donna plus de louanges
à Mlle. Clairon, c'est qu'il ne pouvait se passer d'elle
dans ses ouvrages, et qu'il redoutait son caractère,
tandis qu'il était bien sûr de n'avoir rien à craindre
de Mlle. Dumesnil.' It appears, then, that some respectable judges preferred the spontaneous sublimity
of Dumesnil to the calculated correctness of Diderot's
ideal Clairon.

Garrick
How are we to reconcile the sameness Garrick is
said to have exhibited in certain cases with the spontaneity he certainly approved? Why, very easily—
he accepted the inspirations of the moment, he did not
rely upon them. It may fairly be doubted whether
Dumesnil herself ever went on the stage without
knowing clearly what she intended to do, though she
may have been less scrupulous than Clairon in carry-
Mr.
Jefferson
ing out her exact intentions. Joseph Jefferson, the in-
comparable Rip van Winkle, once remarked to Miss
Mary Anderson that inspiration produces the greatest effects on the stage, but that one cannot afford
to wait for it, and must therefore have everything
regulated in advance in case it should not come.
He himself, therefore, has his ' business ' prearranged
down to pulling off each finger of a glove at a given
Mr. Irving
word of a given speech. I may add that Mr. Irving,

who has gone forth to battle with M. Coquelin on this
very subject of inspiration, is himself (as I am assured
on all hands) scrupulous in repeating night after night
every minutest detail of attitude and gesture.

An often-quoted saying of Baron's places him
clearly on the side of spontaneity. 'Les règles,' he
said, ' défendent d'élever les bras au-dessus de la tête ;
mais si la passion les y porte, ils feront bien. La
passion en sait plus que les règles.' This chimes with
the well-known anecdote of Voltaire tying the hands
of a novice with pack-thread to restrain her exuberance of gesture, but applauding when an irresistible
impulse of passion forced her to burst her bonds. It
is said of Lekain, on the other hand, that ' ses gestes
étaient toujours les mêmes ; apprêtés, compassés et
mesurés géométriquement ; que sur chacun de ses
rôles, il les avait scrupuleusement notés en marge ;
qu'il passait la matinée à les étudier devant une glace,
et que quiconque lui avait vu jouer un rôle, pouvait
annoncer, scène par scène, tous les gestes dont il y
ferait constamment usage.' Lemazurier throws doubt
on this statement, arguing that, were it true, Lekain
would have been a bad actor ; but what ' would have
been ' must yield before what ' was.' Anthony Aston
tells us of Mrs. Verbruggen that ' she was all Art,
and her Acting all acquir'd, but dress'd so nice, it
look'd like Nature. There was not a Look, a Motion,
but what were all design'd ; and these at the same
Word, Period, Occasion, Incident, were every Night,
in the same Character, alike ; and yet all sat charm-
ingly easy on her.' Mrs. Verbruggen, better known

Baron,

*Lema-
zurier, i.
p. 97*

Lekain

*Lema-
zurier, i.
p. 362*

Aston, p. 18

as Mrs. Mountfort, was one of the first actresses of
her time. 'She was Mistress of more variety of
Humour,' says Cibber, ' than I ever knew in any one
Woman Actress.'

Dramatic records abound in instances of great
effects produced ' on the spur of the moment.' One of
the most remarkable, certainly, is Charlotte Cushman's
creation Meg Merrilies. In the season 1840–41, she
was an unknown ' utility ' actress at the Park Theatre,
New York. Braham, the great tenor, was appearing
as Harry Bertram in *Guy Mannering*, when one day
Mrs. Chippendale, who played Meg Merrilies, fell ill.
The part was handed to Miss Cushman about midday,
the intention being that she should read it. When
the evening arrived, however, she knew it by heart.
' Study, dress, &c. had to be the inspiration of the
moment. She had never especially noticed the part
. . . . but as she stood at the side-scene, book in
hand, awaiting her moment of entrance, her ear caught
the dialogue going on upon the stage between two of
the gypsies, in which one says to the other, alluding
to her, " Meg—why, she is no longer what she was ;
she doats," &c. . . . With the words a vivid flash of
insight struck upon her brain. . . . She gave herself
with her usual concentrated energy of purpose to this
conception, and flashed at once upon the stage in
the startling, weird, and terrible manner which we all
so well remember : Braham afterwards came to her
dressing-room and said, " Miss Cushman, I have come
to thank you for the most veritable sensation I have
experienced for a long time. I give you my word

*Charlotte
Cushman*

*Charlotte
Cushman,
p. 15*

when I turned and saw you in that first scene, I felt a cold chill run all over me. Where have you learned to do anything like that?"' Afterwards, no doubt, Miss Cushman greatly elaborated the character, which was the chief triumph of her career ; but the effect of her first performance proves that 'la fureur du premier jet' is not always to be despised.

A most interesting case of momentary inspiration is recorded by Lady Martin, in her account of the first performance of *The Lady of Lyons* :—' As I recalled to Claude, in bitter scorn, his glowing description of his Palace by the Lake of Como, I broke into a paroxysm of hysterical laughter, which came upon me, I suppose, as the natural relief from the intensity of the mingled feelings of anger, scorn, wounded pride and outraged love, by which I found myself carried away. The effect upon the audience was electrical because the impulse was genuine. But well do I remember Mr. Macready's remonstrance with me for yielding to it. It was too daring, he said ; to have failed in it might have ruined the scene (which was true). No one, moreover, should ever, he said, hazard an unrehearsed effect. I could only answer that I could not help it ; that this seemed the only way for my feelings to find vent ; and if the impulse seized me again, again, I feared, I must act the scene in the same way. And often as I have played Pauline, never did the scene fail to bring back the same burst of hysterical emotion ; nor, so far as I know, did any of my critics regard my yielding to it as out of place, or otherwise than true to nature.'

Lady Martin, *Shakespeare's Female Characters, p.* 205

Macready   Macready's rebuke to Miss Faucit is quite in character; for Macready was perhaps the chief of a host
of actors who disprove Diderot's assumption that
'feeling' and 'study' are things incompatible. He was
an uncompromising believer in real emotion—of that
we have had ample proof—and his great intelligence,
combined with his almost morbid habit of introspec-
*Macready
as I knew
him, pp.
27, 50*   tion, gives his judgment unquestionable weight. 'In
reading, as in acting,' he said to Lady Pollock, 'intense
feeling must move the performer; any interruption
that checks the feeling, destroys the power'; and in
the same delightful book we are told that he gave
up the idea of teaching elocution 'with the conviction
that no man could teach feeling; and to teach the
rest without that, would only be to engraft his own
manner upon another.' Yet this double-dyed emotionalist was never tired of insisting on the necessity
for diligent study and minute elaboration of 'tones,
attitudes and looks.' He praises these methods in
other artists; his diary abounds in evidence that he
practised them himself; and independent testimony
from a score of different sources represents him to
have been a very martinet, both to himself and others,
in his insistence on exact pre-arrangement of effects.
What becomes, then, of the supposed antagonism
between sensibility and study?

i. p. 180   A curious passage in the *Correspondence and Table-
Talk* of Benjamin Robert Haydon bears directly on
the point under discussion. Haydon, says his son,
'was once induced by one of the family to go and
Macready see Macready in *Lear.* He sat out the first act and

then went away, saying he could not stand any more
of it. He afterwards ridiculed the whole thing, comparing Macready to a machine wound up to go through
a certain representation, and every night in the same
part performing exactly the same movements and
making exactly the same noises. Edmund Kean, he
maintained, never played the same part twice in the
same way. The same thing was true, he also said, of
Mrs. Siddons. Of John Kemble the machine theory
was always true. Haydon had studied Edmund
Kean, from his first appearance in *Richard III.*, in all
his great parts in his best days. Mr. Lewes, who
allows that he only saw Kean in his later and feebler
days, asserts, on the other hand, that Kean never
trusted to "the inspiration of the moment." This is
probably true of Kean's later period, when his intem-
perate habits obscured his fine genius, and he could no
longer rely upon the advent of the divine afflatus at
the right instant. But Edmund Kean (as he remembered him) and Mrs. Siddons were Haydon's faith.'
The value of this passage lies in Haydon's assertion
that the acting of Kean and Mrs. Siddons used to
vary from night to night. Such variety, as I have
tried to show, is not at all inconsistent with that
assiduous study which George Henry Lewes was
right in declaring to have been characteristic of Kean.
As for Macready, it is hard to understand how, by
seeing him once in one act of *Lear*, Haydon could
discover that he was always the same. It is true
that he was scrupulous in the pre-regulation of all
such details as belong to stage-management, but his

E. Kean

*Mrs. Sid-
dons
Kemble*

*Actors and
Acting,
p. 7*

diaries contain abundant evidence that throughout his career he never (in stage slang) 'put a part to bed,' but was always restlessly experimenting with a view to self-improvement.

Fanny
Kemble

Macready said of Fanny Kemble that she 'did not know the rudiments of her profession'; and if self-control be one of the rudiments the following confession proves that, as she herself puts it, he

Record of a
Girlhood,
ii. p. 86

was 'not far wrong.' 'In the last scene [of *Venice Preserved*],' she writes, 'where poor Belvidera's brain gives way under her despair, and she fancies herself digging for her husband in the earth, and that she at last recovers and seizes him, I intended to utter a piercing scream; this I had not of course rehearsed, not being able to scream deliberately in cold blood, so that I hardly knew, myself, what manner of utterance I should find for my madness. But when the evening came, I uttered shriek after shriek without stopping, and rushing off the stage ran all round the back of the scenes, and was pursuing my way, perfectly unconscious of what I was doing, down the stairs that led out into the street, when I was captured and brought back to my dressing-room and my senses.' This is an excellent instance both of an unrehearsed effect and of inartistic, somnambulistic absorption; for Miss Kemble seems to have had precisely the characteristics which Diderot ascribes to Dumesnil. Her inability to rehearse a scream in cold blood con-

Ante, p. 61

trasts with Rachel's careful 'study of her sobs.' Yet

Rachel

Rachel, too, seems to have been to some extent dependent, in spite of herself, on momentary inspiration.

She was apt to play badly for the first few nights of a new creation ; and on such occasions she said to Houssaye, ' J'enrage, car je me sens enchaînée.' ' Mais tout à coup,' Houssaye continues, ' le dieu l'emportait et elle éclatait en miracles.' *La Comé-dienne, p. 150*

Almost all the artists whom I have personally consulted allow that within due limits they readily avail themselves of inspiration, and most condemn as false in principle the too rigorous sameness, even down to the movement of a particular finger at a particular word, which a few actors laboriously cultivate. Many very happy effects have certainly been suggested by the spirit of the scene and produced on the spur of the moment—perhaps never to be reproduced. 'The late Mrs. Charles Kean told me,' writes Mr. Frank Harvey, ' that while playing at the Princess's Theatre she once made a great sensation in a moment of nervous excitement, and afterwards could not even remember what she had done, far less reproduce it.' Mrs. C. Kean

Salvini is emphatic in his assertion that the finest effects are often unpremeditated, and that such inspirations can sometimes be seized and reproduced. As to the respective merits of study and inspiration, he expresses himself in almost the identical words used by Garrick in his criticism of Clairon. I am assured by several observers that Salvini varies very much in his 'business ' from night to night, even to the extent of delivering a particular speech now up the stage, now down, standing one night, sitting the next, and on the third, perhaps, lolling on a divan. Robson, too (as I learn on the authority Salvini *Ante, p. 180* Robson of his widow), was very erratic in his movements on the stage.

Mrs.
Bancroft

'I have often,' writes Mrs. Bancroft, 'been inspired to introduce on the spur of the moment a new gesture or a new reading of certain lines. . . . The voice must be guided by the feelings and love of the subject. Emotion has a wide range, and the heart can produce many notes. These I play upon as the fit seizes me. Mr. Bancroft adds that on the first night of *Sweethearts* Mrs. Bancroft spoke Jenny Northcott's last line with a delicate pathos of intonation which she never

Mr. Vezin

afterwards entirely 'recaptured.' Mr. Hermann Vezin, both in theory and in practice, leaves a wide margin for variation in gesture. One gesture, he says, is true to your way of feeling the situation on one night, another on another. He condemns, for instance, the three solemn taps on the brow with which Charles Kean always preluded the line, ' In my mind's eye, Horatio '; and he relates some curious examples of Frédérick Lemaître's variability in this respect. 'Je

M. Lam-
bert

suis capable,' writes M. Albert Lambert, 'quelque empoigné que je sois par la situation, de me rappeler l'accent que j'ai trouvé, mais pas toujours de le reproduire ; et c'est alors que je m'aperçois que la seule vraie sensibilité trouve la corde vibrante de l'effet. Le hasard m'a servi souvent, et l'inspiration de mes camarades aussi ; et à ce propos, le plus grand des plaisirs est de jouer la comédie avec de grands comédiens—j'entends des penseurs, et non des acteurs. Leurs regards, leurs silences, leurs pensées vous donnent des répliques mystérieuses et de soudaines inspirations.' Of M. Mounet Sully, again, M. Larcher, founding, evidently, on personal confessions, writes, 'Il est en état d'improvisation constante.' Mr. Beerbohm Tree, at the commencement of his career, used to force himself always to make a given gesture at a given word, but was taught by experience to regard the practice as useless and embarrassing. Mr. Clayton related to me an amusing yet really valuable instance of inspiration. Salome, in *Dandy Dick*, has just read from the *Times* the paragraph announcing the Dean's munificent offer of 1,000*l.* to the Minster Restoration Fund 'on condition that seven other donors come forward, each with the like sum.' ' And will they ?' cries Sheba eagerly ; whereupon the Dean, who has been standing with his back to the audience, turns with an unctuous yet sickly smile, and replies, ' My darling—times are bad, but one never knows.' This smile was an inspiration. For some time after the production of the play Mr. Clayton used to speak the line gravely and meditatively, without producing any effect. One evening the smile—a really admirable trait—came to his lips almost before he knew what he was doing. The audience rose to it immediately, and from that day forward the speech, thus accentuated, remained one of the most successful in the piece. A somewhat similar story is told of Mr. John Hare. He was playing the bibulous Baron Croodle on the first night of *The Money-spinner*, when by chance a champagne-cork was heard to pop behind the scenes. Mr. Hare had the presence of mind to let his face light up with an expression of rapturous

Marginal notes: M. Mounet, *Revue d'Art Dramatique*, March 1, 1887 — Mr. Beerbohm Tree — Mr. Clayton — Mr. John Hare

O

anticipation ; and the result was so good that the incident was afterwards repeated every evening.

On the whole, there is every reason to believe that, within due limits, momentary impulse plays an important and legitimate part upon the stage. But it is none the less evident that the actor who 'trusts to inspiration' in the sense of going on the stage unprepared and uncertain of his own intentions, deserves the very hardest things that MM. Diderot and Coquelin can say of him. I may pick up a five-pound note in the street to-morrow ; but I should be a fool to leave my purse at home on the chance.

CHAPTER XIII.

TO RESUME.

IN ordering this discussion, I have had a double difficulty to contend with, as the reader may by this time have discovered to his cost. In the first place, there were two questions at issue—a question of fact and a question of theory : do actors feel? and ought they to feel ? In the second place, I had not the advantage of starting from an unencumbered base and building up my theory in my own way by a straightforward synthesis of evidence. The issue had been obscured (as it seemed to me) by rash overstatements on both sides, and by a general failure to recognise and define the comparatively few points on which rational dispute was possible. Thus my exposition was necessarily mingled with controversy, and I fear the mixture has not thoroughly clarified. If exhaustion have not supervened upon the reader's bewilderment, a brief recapitulation may help him to find his bearings.

Acting is of all the arts the most purely imitative. In this respect it stands at the opposite pole from music, with sculpture, painting, poetry, in intermediate positions. Music deals almost entirely in what may be called sound-patterns, which have no prototypes

O 2

in external nature. Poetry, and indeed all literary art, leans in the same direction. Its matter may or may not be imitative; its medium must be a more or less rhythmic succession of sounds, which does not depend for its attractiveness on its resemblance to anything under the sun. Painting, in these latter days, tends more and more to the condition of colour-music, the very vocabularies of the two arts being, it appears, interchangeable. Even sculpture, without entirely deserting its function, may present a mere arabesque of curves and surfaces. But acting is imitative or it is nothing. It may borrow from all the arts in turn—from the arts of speech, of song, of colour, of form; but imitation is its differentia. Acting *is* imitation; when it ceases to be imitation it ceases to be acting and becomes something else—oratory perhaps, perhaps ballet-dancing or posturing. Everyone knows that the actor is not necessarily a mere copyist of nature; he may sing, for example, or he may talk alexandrines; but he must always preserve a similarity in dissimilarity; he must always imitate, though we may permit him to steep his imitation, so to speak, in a more or less conventional atmosphere. 'He plays naturally,' or, in other words, 'He imitates well,' is our highest formula of praise even for the operatic tenor or the French tragedian, who may not deliver a single word or tone exactly as it would be uttered in real life.

The actor, then, is a man who, through the medium of his own body, imitates the manners and the passions of other men. We are all actors in rudiment,

the tendency to such imitation being part of the mechanism of animated nature. That is why the stage
is besieged by incompetent aspirants, the general
tendency being easily mistaken for special aptitude.
Conversely, I believe, that is why some theorists seek
to exclude acting from the dignity of art. They
ignore the amount of labour and thought required to
transmute, not only the general tendency, but even a
very special aptitude, into accomplished mastery.

By far the greater part of the imitation of man by
man which takes place off the stage is totally un-
concerned with emotion. In real life the emotions of
others are precisely what we do *not* imitate. A child
learns to speak, to walk, to sing by imitating ·its
elders : it wails before its eyes are fairly opened to
the world. We are all conscious of a tendency to
mimic the tics and mannerisms of our neighbours—
their gait, their voice, their accent ; but the mere
muscular copying of emotional manifestations never
occurs, except for purposes of ridicule. The grief
or laughter of another may seize‾ and overmaster
us, through the action of sympathy, though we may
know nothing of its cause ; but this is not imitation :
it is infection. It may be said that all imitation
which is not absolutely deliberate partakes of the
nature of infection. True ; but the infection of feeling
has this peculiarity, that it is *not imitative*. We weep
our own tears, we laugh our own laughter, without
the smallest conscious or unconscious tendency to
reproduce the particular forms which these paroxysms
assume in the person who has 'set us off.' Therefore

I think there is a clear distinction between mimicking tricks or habits and yielding to emotional contagion. Roughly speaking, the one is an affair of the surface, the other of the centres.

The manners and passions of his fellow-men form, as we have seen, the actor's province. Over part of this domain unemotional imitation will carry him safely. The reproduction of manners, in themselves, is effected by a mere extension of that instinct which makes children the ' sedulous apes ' of their elders, and causes some of us, even in maturity, to stammer after conversing with a stammerer and to wink and twitch after seeing a victim to St. Vitus's dance. In all characters there is a greater or less element of manner, so that in all characters this instinct of mere imitation is brought into play. A large part of every impersonation is, and must be, as mechanical as the putting on of a wig or the painting of crows'-feet under the eyes. But comparatively few dramatic characters consist of manners alone. It is passion that interests and moves us ; therefore the reproduction of passion is the actor's highest and most essential task. By what methods, then, can this reproduction be most fitly accomplished ?

The external manifestations of passion consist, on analysis, of changes in the face, the limbs, or the organs of speech, many of which can be mechanically imitated with more or less precision, just as one can imitate the limp of a cripple or an Irishman's brogue. For example, we can all contort our faces into the semblance of weeping, we can smile and laugh at will (though the voluntary laugh is apt to be a lugubrious effort), we can sob, we can tremble, we can gnash and grind the teeth, not quite convincingly perhaps, but so that an observer can easily guess what emotion we are simulating. On the other hand, some of the symptoms of those passions which tend to express themselves immediately, forcibly, and unmistakably —the passions of grief and joy, terror and fury— cannot be imitated by the mere action of the will upon the muscles and tissues. No one can blush and turn pale at will ; some actors, as we have seen reason to believe, can shed tears at a moment's notice and without any real or imaginary cause ; but this faculty is not common, and is the result of long practice. These involuntary symptoms, however, are of such a nature as to be almost imperceptible on the stage. If the more obvious traits are vividly reproduced, a theatrical audience is ready enough to take tears, blushes, and pallor upon trust. It is undeniable, then, that for the practical purposes of dramatic presentation, the symptoms of passion can be mechanically mimicked with tolerable precision, and there is no reason to doubt that exceptional artists have attained astonishing skill in such mimicry.

It is certain, however, that the faculty of mechanically mimicking the ebullitions of passion with anything like deceptive precision is a very rare one. We have seen that our innate mimetic tendency does not generally exercise itself upon these phenomena ; perhaps for no more recondite reason than that they are of exceptional occurrence and do not force them-

selves on our observation with the importunacy of
habitual actions. Be this as it may, it is clear that
the mechanical mimicking of passions on the stage is
not, like the mimicking of manners, a mere extension
of an inborn instinct. On the other hand, we have
also seen that the paroxysms of passion tend to communicate themselves to those not primarily affected,
through that subtle contagion which we call sympathy. Little Mabel breaks her favourite doll and
howls piteously over the remains. Her elder brother,
Jack, though his sex and his years raise him far above
the weakness of doll-worship, nay, though he may
have a dim sense of Rochefoucauldian satisfaction in
Mabel's misfortune, will very probably yell in con-
cert, as lustily as though the sorrow were his own.
He certainly does not suffer anything like Mabel's
agony of soul ; in a sense he cannot properly be said
to suffer at all ; and still less can it be maintained that
he deliberately mimics his sister. All we can say is
that by the mysterious action of sympathy Mabel's
grief acts upon Jack's nerve-centres and begets in
them a condition so analogous to her own that it
results in similar outward manifestations. The difference between the two states might be tested by
the exhibition of a counter-irritant. A chocolate-
cream will probably dry Jack's eyes as if by magic;
while a wilderness of lollipops will leave Mabel in-
consolable. In this sympathetic contagion we have
an instrument provided by nature for supplying the
deficiencies of our power of mechanical mimicry in
respect to the subtler symptoms of passion. The

poet—say Shakespeare—fecundates the imagination of the actor—say Salvini—so that it bodies forth the great passion-quivering phantom of Othello. In the act of representation this phantom is, as it were, superimposed upon the real man. The phantom Othello suffers, and the nerve-centres of the man Salvini thrill in response. The blood courses through his veins, his eyes are clouded with sorrow or blaze with fury, his lips tremble, the muscles of his throat contract, the passion of the moment informs him to the finger-tips, and his portrayal of a human soul in agony is true to the minutest detail. His suffering may stand to Othello's in the quantitative relation of Jack's grief to Mabel's ; but, so far as it goes, it cannot be called other than real.

The anti-emotionalists would have the actor abjure, at any rate in the moment of performance, the aid of this sympathetic contagion. It is too dearly bought, they argue. The accomplished player should be able mechanically to mimic all symptoms of emotion which are of any use in creating illusion in the audience, and he must run no risk of becoming extravagant, inarticulate, or feeble, by reason of the too vehement disturbance of his own nerve-centres. The emotionalists, as I understand their position, maintain that the mechanical mimicry of feeling, even at its best, lacks the clear ring of truth, and that in yielding to the sympathetic contagion the accomplished actor does not in reality run any of the risks on which their opponents are so fond of dwelling.

The two questions, then, which we have had to

consider in this discussion—do actors feel? and ought they to feel?—may be restated thus: Do actors habitually yield to the sympathetic contagion? and do the greatest actors—those who have most powerfully affected their audiences—admit or reject this method?

Chapters i., ii., iii.

My first three chapters were purely preliminary. I described the methods of investigation I had pursued; traced, historically, the genesis of Diderot's *Paradoxe*; and tried to narrow the issue by analysing the different meanings attributed in the *Paradoxe* to the term 'sensibility,' and rejecting some of them as unfair or irrelevant. The investigation proper began

Chap. iv.

with the fourth chapter. In it we found that the shedding of tears—one of the most palpable symptoms of pathetic emotion—is common, and even habitual, on the stage. We learned from Cicero and Quintilian that the Roman actors frequently wept; and we ascertained, in most cases on unimpeachable evidence, that tears have been shed on the stage by Garrick, Mrs. Cibber, Barry, Peg Woffington, Mrs. Pritchard, Mrs. Siddons, Miss O'Neill, Miss Fanny Kemble, Mlle. Champmeslé, Mlle. Duclos, Quinault-Dufresne, Mlle. Gaussin, Frédérick Lemaître, Madame Dorval, Miss Neilson, Charlotte Cushman, Samuel Phelps, Benjamin Webster, Salvini, Mr. and Mrs. Bancroft, Mr. and Mrs. Kendal, Mr. Irving, Miss Ellen Terry, Madame Sarah Bernhardt, Miss Mary Anderson, Miss Alma Murray, Miss Achurch, Miss Clara Morris, Mr. Wilson Barrett, Mr. Beerbohm

Tree, Mr. John Clayton, Mr. Hermann Vezin, Mr. Howe, Miss Bateman, Mr. Lionel Brough, and several others. It would not have cost much trouble to extend this list almost indefinitely, but it seems to me sufficient as it stands, both in numbers and in authority. The frequency of real weeping on the *Chap. v.* stage being thus established, I had next to admit that tears can, in certain cases, be mechanically produced, and that they do not, therefore, afford conclusive evidence of any particular emotional state. In order to show that they are not, as a rule, so fallacious as the anti-emotionalists argue, and at the same time to prove that there is a close analogy between personal and mimetic emotion, I collected, in my fifth chapter, numerous instances of the mingling and (in M. Coquelin's phrase) ' kneading together ' of the two states, which we found to coalesce indistinguishably, sometimes to the advantage, sometimes to the detriment, of the actor's performance. On the other hand, in Chapter Six, we found scanty evidence of any *Chap. vi.* tendency to mimic in cold blood particular ebullitions of emotion, whether observed or experienced, and no proof whatever that unemotional mimicry is more effective than emotional acting. In the following *Chap. vii.* chapter, treating of laughter as the characteristic expression of joyful emotion, and thus the natural antithesis to tears, we found a rather wide divergence of testimony. Some actors declare themselves highly susceptible to the contagion of their character's mirth, others (of no less authority) are equally positive in asserting their laughter to be always a deliberate

simulative effort.   I confess myself unable to suggest
any satisfactory reason why the contagion of merriment should be less potent and universal than the contagion of tears.   Can it be that there is a pessimistic
bias in human nature, rendering men, on the average,
less prone to joyous than to mournful emotion ?

Here let me interrupt this recapitulation to point
out a fact which is apt to be overlooked.   In the
course of my interviews with the leading artists of
to-day, I have more than once mentioned, say, to X.
—an emphatic emotionalist—that a fellow-artist, Z.,
had declared himself of the same opinion ; whereupon X. would shrug his (or her) shoulders scepti-
cally and remark, ' Oh, Z.!—I don't believe *he* ever
felt anything in his life ! '   The doubt in these cases
sprang from the common error of thinking that
sensitiveness to what we have called the imaginative contagion presupposes unusual sensibility in the
ordinary affairs of life.   A little consideration will
show us that the fact is not so.   The executioner in
Thackeray blubbered over *The Sorrows of Werther* ;
and no one will deny that this is a touch of nature.
To take an example from real life, Macaulay, who
met his personal sorrows in no unmanly spirit, could
weep by the hour over a trashy novel.   We must
all have known people, stoical enough in their own
troubles, and perhaps even hard-hearted towards the
sufferings of others, who would yet become maudlin
over the imagined sorrows of a personage in fiction
or on the stage.   Thus the actor who owns himself
affected by the emotions of his character—the super-

imposed phantom of his imagination—does not thereby lay any claim to exceptional tenderness of heart
in the ordinary relations of life. In that respect, I
imagine, actors are very much like other men. Diderot,
as we have seen, found them 'caustic, cold, selfish, *Ante. p.* 34
alive to our absurdities rather than touched by our
misfortunes.' This character certainly does not apply
to the players of our nation and time, whose large
and ready charity proves that ' they know what 'tis to
pity and be pitied.' But even if Diderot were absolutely just in his general assertion of the heartless-
ness of actors, we should still have no difficulty in
believing them susceptible to emotional contagion
from the phantoms of their imagination.

Continuing my summary, I pass to Chapter *Chap. viii.*
Eight. Here we ascertained that three symptoms of
acute feeling, which are utterly beyond the control
of the will—blushing, pallor, and perspiration—commonly, and even habitually, accompany the stage-
emotion of the greatest artists. In this, it seems to
me, we have proof positive that mimetic emotion is
not, as some people argue, a state of mere vague
unspecialised excitement, but is closely analogous to
the emotion of real life. In the next chapter we *Chap. ix.*
inquired into the practice, attributed to several great
artists, of mechanically mobilising the nerve-centres
by means of that reaction from external manifestations of passion which Hartmann describes as ' autosuggestion.' This proceeding, in various forms, we
found to be fairly common ; while the habit of mental
concentration upon a part during, and even for some

time before, the period of performance, proved to be
still more general.   The rationale of these practices
is obvious enough.   The one assists the actor to
clothe himself, as it were, in the phantom of his
imagination, and to keep himself thoroughly en-
veloped in it ; the other heightens the sensitiveness
of his organism to contagion from the emotions of
Chap. x. his personage.   The next chapter was devoted to
an inquiry into the multiplex action of the mind
whereby the accomplished actor is enabled to remain
master of himself even in the very paroxysm of
passion.   I was able to adduce many cases in which
double and treble strata of mental activity were
clearly distinguishable, but very few examples of that
total and somnambulistic absorption in a part which
the anti-emotionalists assume to be the normal
Chap. xi. condition of the emotional actor.   The succeeding
chapter touched upon the question of long runs. We
saw reason, on the one hand, to reject Diderot's
opinion that an actor must gain by reiterating a
character until his playing becomes entirely automatic, and to believe, on the other hand, that an
actor may repeat a character indefinitely without
degenerating into automatism, if only he takes care
to allow himself proper intervals of rest and change
between the performances of any one part.   Finally,
Chap. xii. in Chapter Twelve, we ' Reasoned high Of fate, free
will, foreknowledge absolute '—I trust the reader will
not complete the quotation, adding 'And found no
end, in wandering mazes lost.' We learned that
some actors are artistic Calvinists, insisting on rigor-

ous predestination of every detail of position, attitude, gesture, and inflexion ; while others, the Arminians of the stage, leave a wide margin for impulse, spontaneity, free-will. The latter sect is probably the more numerous and influential ; but we also ascertained that the ' foreknowledge absolute ' of the necessitarians is by no means inconsistent with the keenest susceptibility to the emotional influence of their characters.

At the very outset of this inquiry, I insisted on the distinction between the simple or primary emotions —grief, joy, terror, &c.—and the secondary or complex and habitual emotions—love, hatred, jealousy, &c.—which have no immediate and characteristic outward symptoms, and are rather to be called attitudes of mind. No one denies, I think, that the primary emotions of an imagined character do in fact tend to communicate themselves to the nerve-centres of the actor, and to affect his organs of expression. Let me add, parenthetically, that it is surely illogical to deny the ' reality ' of this mimetic emotion, since all emotion, except that which arises from instant physical pleasure or pain, is due to the action of the imagination upon the nerve-centres. This, however, is a mere question of nomenclature. Be it real or unreal, this mimetic emotion tends, in the great majority of cases, to come into play ; and the actor who avails himself of it clearly works on the line of least resistance. The anti-emotionalists must prove that this straightforward course is beset with the most

Ante, p. 37

fatal pitfalls ere they can hope to induce actors to
follow the roundabout route, repressing the action of
the imagination and cultivating mechanical mimicry.
I have tried to show that the pitfalls from which
the anti-emotionalists recoil are either quite imaginary or easily to be avoided. On the other hand,
the more we look into the matter, the less are we
inclined to believe that even the greatest virtuoso
of mechanical mimicry can attain to the subtle and
absolute truth of imitation which is possible to the
actor who combines artistically controlled sensibility
with perfect physical means of expression. 'Raised
or lowered by the twentieth part of the quarter of a
tone,' says Diderot, the utterances of feeling 'ring
false.' But is it not just the intervention of imaginative sympathy that enables the actor to produce
and reproduce this delicately true vibration? There
is no doubt that the imagination can readily bring
about minute yet expressive changes, muscular and
vascular, which the unaided action of the will is
powerless to effect. Blushing and pallor are the
chief of these, but there must be many others. Darwin notes that when two dogs fight together in play
(that is, when they imagine and act the emotion of
anger) their hair at once bristles up, just as in actual
warfare. This is a type of many similar phenomena
in the human economy. And it must not be supposed
that these minute changes do not contribute appre-
ciably to the illusion. We may not consciously note
a blush, a sudden pallor, a particular quiver of the
lip, distension of the nostril, or corrugation of the

Ante, p. 25

*Expression
of the
Emotions,
p.* 102

brow ; but they produce their effect nevertheless.
Mr. Kendal once suggested to me what I think a
luminous illustration of the difference between mechanically simulated and imaginatively experienced
emotion. 'A sign-painter,' he said, 'takes a pot of
crude vermilion, and daubs the red coat of the Duke
of Wellington or the Marquis of Granby. It is un-
deniably red, and yet somehow it is all wrong. But
look into a red robe painted by Rossetti or Holman
Hunt, and you will find it composed of a hundred
different hues, which blend, at the proper distance,
into a true and living whole.' To translate the illustration into musical terms, a mechanically mimicked
utterance of emotion is like a note without its har-
monics. The analogy may be fanciful, but I do not
think it is wholly misleading.

In the foregoing pages there are, no doubt, errors
of analysis and of inference which have escaped my
ken. On the other hand, no one knows better than
I that the subject of mimetic emotion is full of
subtleties and intricacies into which I have not
penetrated. Some day, perhaps, a better-equipped
psychologist may thread the maze to its inmost
recesses. Meanwhile, in taking leave of what has
been to me a fascinating inquiry, I cannot but hope
that it may aid the contending forces in a lingering
and somewhat futile controversy to arrive at a clearer
understanding of the true points at issue than they
have hitherto attained. If each party fully realised
its own and its adversaries' position, I believe a treaty

P

of peace would very soon be signed.   It was drafted by Shakespeare three centuries ago, when, through the mouth of Prince Hamlet, he counselled the players of his day to acquire and beget a temperance even in the very torrent, tempest, and whirlwind of passion.

APPENDIX

—◦◦—

QUESTIONS ON THE ART OF ACTING,

FORMULATED ON BEHALF OF THE EDITOR OF 'LONGMANS' MAGAZINE,'

BY WILLIAM ARCHER.

FOREWORD.

A FRIENDLY controversy between M. Coquelin and Mr. Henry Irving has recently revived a discussion started by Diderot in his *Paradoxe sur le Comédien.* 'To feel, or not to feel?—that is the question.' Diderot and M. Coquelin maintain that 'sensibility' is the bane of acting ; that even in the storm and whirlwind of passion an actor must be cool, calm, and collected ; that he must simulate

> Tears in his eyes, distraction in 's aspect,
> A broken voice.

and so forth ; but that his eyes must in reality be dry, and that the break in his voice must be simply 'put on' like his wig or his rouge. In short, Diderot flatly contradicts the Horatian maxim thus rendered by Churchill—

> But, spite of all the criticising elves,
> Those who would make us feel must feel themselves.

Mr. Irving, on the other hand, maintains (and he claims the great authority of Talma on his side) that sensibility is the

P 2

prime requisite of great acting. ' The actor,' he says, ' who combines the electric force of a strong personality with a mastery of the resources of his art, must have a greater power over his audiences than the passionless actor who gives a most artistic simulation of the emotions he never experiences.' And again : ' If tears be produced at the actor's will and under his control, they are true art ; and happy is the actor who numbers them among his gifts.' Some writers on the subject have drawn a distinction between the *conception* and the *execution* of a character, admitting that sensibility may aid the actor to conceive and elaborate a part, but arguing that it must be strictly repressed during the performance. Other shades and refinements of opinion need not be enumerated here.

What is clearly essential to any fruitful discussion of the subject is a wide collection of the individual experiences of actors and actresses. Diderot's argument was purely *à priori*, though he eked it out with a few scraps of anecdote. Mr. Irving and M. Coquelin rely almost entirely on their own experiences ; and the opinions of only two actors, however distinguished, cannot be conclusive, especially when they contradict each other. No attempt has hitherto been made to compare the experiences of any considerable number of dramatic artists ; yet such a comparison must surely form the basis of all profitable argument.

The editor of *Longmans' Magazine* has commissioned me to collect and systematise the views on this matter of the leading actors and actresses of the day. I have accordingly drawn up a series of questions bearing upon what I conceive to be the true point at issue ; and I confidently appeal to the courtesy of my readers to assist me in an inquiry, the result of which can scarcely fail to be of interest to all who care for dramatic art. I have ventured to add one or two questions which do not bear directly upon the subject of Diderot's *Paradoxe* but are of importance in connection with other points in the theory of acting. This species of cut-and-dried interrogatory, however, is at best an unsatisfactory mode of eliciting information, and I beg that those artists who are kind enough to respond to my request will not hold themselves bound to answer these questions and no more, but will use the utmost freedom in giving me their views and experiences. It will naturally add to the value of opinions and anecdotes if I am allowed to attach names to them ; but I shall scrupulously observe any condition to the contrary.

I am aware that no one actor or actress can possibly answer *all* the following questions from personal experience, but I believe that everyone will find *some* points suggested on which he (or she) can throw light.

If any artist who may have been inadvertently omitted from my list will favour me with his (or her) name and address, I will at once forward a question-form to be filled up.

I.

In moving situations, do tears come to your eyes ? Do they come unbidden ? Can you call them up and repress them at will ? In delivering pathetic speeches does your voice break of its own accord ? Or do you deliberately simulate a broken voice ? Supposing that, in the same situation, you on one night shed real tears and speak with a genuine ' lump in your throat,' and on the next night simulate these affections without physically experiencing them : on which occasion should you expect to produce the greater effect upon your audience ?

II.

' When Macready played Virginius, after burying his loved daughter, he confessed that his real experience gave a new force to his acting in the most pathetic situations of

the play.'   Have you any analogous experience to relate?
Has a personal sorrow (whether recent or remote) ever influenced your acting in a situation which recalled the painful
circumstances to your mind?   If so, was the influence, in
your opinion, for good or for ill?   And what was the effect
upon the audience?

III.

In scenes of laughter (for instance, Charles Surface's part
in the screen scene, or Lady Teazle's part in the quarrel
with Sir Peter), do you feel genuine amusement?   Or is
your merriment entirely assumed?   Have you ever laughed
on the stage until the tears ran down your face? or been so
overcome with laughter as to have a difficulty in continuing
your part?   And in either of these cases, what has been the
effect upon the audience?   [N.B.—These questions do not
refer to laughter caused by chance blunders or other unrehearsed incidents, but solely to laughter which forms part of
the business of the play.   A question as to laughter of the
former kind will be found in Section XI.]

IV.

Do you ever blush when representing bashfulness,
modesty, or shame? or turn pale in scenes of terror? or
grow purple in the face in scenes of rage? or have you observed these physical manifestations in other artists?   On
leaving the stage after a scene of terror or of rage, can you
at once repress the tremor you have been exhibiting, and
restore your nerves and muscles to their normal quietude?

V.

A distinguished actor informs me that he generally perspires freely while acting, but that the perspiration varies,
not so much with the physical exertion gone through as with
the emotion experienced.   On nights when he was not
' feeling the part,' he has played Othello ' without turning a

hair,' though his physical effort was at least as great as on nights when he was bathed in perspiration. Does your experience tally with this? Do you find the fatigue of playing a part directly proportionate to the physical exertion demanded by it? or dependent on other causes?

VI.

Have you ever played a comic part when labouring under severe sorrow or mental depression? If so, have you produced less effect than usual upon the audience? or more effect? Have you ever played a tragic part while enjoying abnormal exhilaration of spirits? If so, how has your playing been affected?

VII.

It used to be said of a well-known actor that he put on in the morning the character he was to play at night : that on days when he was to play Richard III. he was truculent, cynical, and cruel, while on days when he was to play Mercutio and Benedick he would be all grace, humour, and courtesy. Are you conscious of any such tendency in yourself? or have you observed it in others? In the green-room, between the acts, have you any tendency to preserve the voice and manner of the character you are playing? or have you observed such a tendency in others?

VIII.

G. H. Lewes relates how Macready, as Shylock, used to shake a ladder violently before going on for the scene with Tubal, in order to get up 'the proper state of white heat'; also how Liston was overheard 'cursing and spluttering to himself, as he stood at the side scene waiting to go on in a scene of comic rage.' Have you experienced any difficulty in thus 'striking twelve at once'? If so, how do you overcome it?

IX.

Can you give any examples of the two or more strata of consciousness, or lines of thought, which must co-exist in your mind while acting? Or, in other words, can you describe and illustrate how one part of your mind is intent on the character, while another part is watching the audience, and a third (perhaps) given up to some pleasant or unpleasant recollection or anticipation in your private life?

X.

Does your personal feeling (such as love, hatred, respect, scorn) towards the actor or actress with whom you happen to be playing affect your performance? If so, in what way? Should you play Romeo better if you were in love with your Juliet than if she were quite indifferent to you? And if you happened to dislike or despise her, how would that influence your acting?

XI.

Diderot tells how Lekain, in a scene of violent emotion, saw an actress's diamond ear-ring lying on the stage, and had presence of mind enough to kick it to the wing instead of treading on it. Can you relate any similar instances of presence of mind? And should you regard them as showing that the actor is personally unmoved by the situation in which he is figuring? Have you ever suffered from inability to control laughter at some chance blunder or unrehearsed incident? And do you find less or greater difficulty in controlling it when you are absorbed in a part than when you are comparatively unmoved? Are you apt to be thrown off the rails (so to speak) by trifling sounds among the audience (a cough or a sneeze), or by slight noises which reach your ear from behind the scenes, or from the street?

XII.

With reference to long runs : Does frequent repetition induce callousness to the emotions of a part ? Do you continue to improve during a certain number of representations and then remain stationary or deteriorate? Or do you go on elaborating a part throughout a long run ? Or do you improve in some respects and deteriorate in others ? In your own opinion, do you act better on (say) the tenth night than on the first? and on the fiftieth than on the tenth ? Do the emotions of a part 'grip' you more forcibly on one night than on another ? If so, is there any corresponding difference in your 'grip' on your audience? [This is a re-statement in more general terms of the last question in Section I.] Have you ever over-rehearsed a part, as an athlete over-trains? Have you ever played a part until it has become nauseous to you ? If so, have you noticed any diminution of its effect upon your audience?

XIII.

In scenes of emotion in real life, whether you are a participant in them (e.g. the death-bed of a relative) or a casual on-looker (e.g. a street accident), do you consciously note effects for subsequent use on the stage? Or can you ever trace an effect used on the stage to some phase of such a real-life experience automatically registered in your memory ?

XIV.

Do you ever yield to sudden inspirations of accent or gesture occurring in the moment of performance ? And are you able to note and subsequently reproduce such inspirations ? Have you ever produced a happy effect by pure chance or by mistake, and then incorporated it permanently in your performance ?

XV.

Do you act with greater satisfaction to yourself in characters which are consonant with your own nature (as you conceive it) than in characters which are dissonant and perhaps antipathetic? And in which class of characters have you met with most success? Does your liking or dislike for—your belief or disbelief in—a play as a whole affect your acting in it?

XVI.

Do you ever find yourself disturbed and troubled by the small conventions of the stage? In other words, is the thread of your emotion broken by the necessity for 'asides, or for giving a stage kiss instead of a real one, a stage buffet instead of a genuine knock-down blow? In the fight in *Macbeth* or *Richard III.*, do you feel hampered by the necessity for counting the cuts and thrusts? Or in flinging away the goblet in *Hamlet*, are you disturbed by having to aim it so that it may be caught by the prompter? Is your hilarity at a stage banquet more convincing to the audience when the champagne is real than when you are quaffing toast and water?

XVII.

In the conception and make-up of a 'character-part,' do you generally (or do you ever) imitate some individual whom you have seen and studied? Or do you piece together a series of observations, reproducing this man's nose, that man's whiskers, the gestures and mannerisms of a third, the voice and accent of a fourth? Or do you construct a purely imaginary figure, no single trait of which you can refer to any individual model?

QUESTIONS SUR L'ART DU COMÉDIEN,

FORMULÉES À LA DEMANDE DU DIRECTEUR DE
'LONGMANS' MAGAZINE,'

PAR WILLIAM ARCHER.

AVANT-PROPOS.

UN débat amical qui s'est élevé récemment entre M. Coquelin et M. Irving a ravivé la discussion jadis provoquée par Diderot dans son *Paradoxe sur le Comédien.* Etre ou n'être pas ému? voilà la question. Diderot et M. Coquelin affirment que la sensibilité est la perte de l'acteur; qu'au sein même des orages et des tourbillons de la passion, l'acteur doit rester froid, calme, et maître de lui ; qu'il doit simuler et les larmes et la voix brisée par l'émotion, etc. etc. mais qu'en réalité ses yeux doivent rester secs et que le brisement de sa voix doit être tout aussi emprunté que sa perruque et son rouge. En résumé, Diderot contredit absolument la maxime d'Horace :

> Si vis me flere, dolendum est
> Primum ipsi tibi.

D'un autre côté, M. Irving soutient (et il s'appuie sur la grande autorité de Talma) que la sensibilité est le principal élément du talent d'un grand acteur. ' L'acteur,' dit-il, ' qui réunit la puissance communicative d'une forte individualité avec la possession pleine et entière de toutes les ressources de son art, doit avoir une plus grande prise sur son auditoire que l'acteur sans passion qui simule avec art les émotions qu'il n'a jamais éprouvées.' Et encore : 'Si un acteur a le pouvoir de verser des larmes à son gré, il a un des secrets du

grand art. et heureux est celui qui possède ce don précieux.'
Quelques écrivains ont établi une distinction entre la *concep-tion* et l'*exécution* d'un rôle, reconnaissant que la sensibilité
peut aider un acteur à concevoir et à élaborer son person-
nage, mais ajoutant qu'elle doit être strictement réprimée·à
la représentation. Nous n'énumérerons pas ici toutes les
nuances et les distinctions subtiles qui peuvent exister à ce
sujet.

Pour qu'une discussion sur ces points intéressants soit
fructueuse, l'essentiel est de réunir en grand nombre les
résultats de l'expérience personnelle des acteurs et des
actrices. La thèse soutenue par Diderot n'était qu'une argu-
mentation *à priori*, bien qu'il l'ait ' illustrée ' ça et là de
quelques anecdotes. M. Irving et M. Coquelin s'en rap-
portent presque entièrement à leur propre expérience ; et
d'ailleurs, l'opinion de deux acteurs seulement, si distingués
qu'ils soient, ne saurait être concluante, surtout quand ils se
contredisent ! On n'a point essayé jusqu'ici de recueillir et
de comparer les expériences d'un grand nombre d'acteurs,
et pourtant c'est cette comparaison seule qui pourrait fournir
la base d'un débat profitable.

Le directeur de *Longmans' Magazine* m'a chargé de
recueillir les idées émises sur ce sujet par les acteurs et
actrices le plus en évidence aujourd'hui, et d'en tirer une
conclusion. En conséquence, j'ai rassemblé une série de
questions portant sur ce que je considère comme le véritable
point en litige, et je fais appel avec confiance à la courtoisie
de mes lecteurs pour m'aider dans une enquête dont le
résultat ne peut manquer d'être fort intéressant pour tous
ceux qui se soucient d'art dramatique. Je me suis aventuré
à ajouter une ou deux questions qui n'ont pas un rapport
direct avec le *Paradoxe* de Diderot, mais qui ne sont pas
sans importance dans la question de l'art du comédien.
Cette sorte d'interrogatoire, si sec et si bref, ne saurait être
qu'une façon fort peu satisfaisante d'obtenir des informations,

et je demande aux artistes qui seront assez bons pour répondre à ma requête, de ne pas limiter leur réponse aux questions posées, mais d'user de la plus grande liberté en me communiquant leurs vues et leurs sentiments. Je n'ai pas besoin de dire que s'il m'est permis d'ajouter des noms aux opinions et anecdotes qui me seront ainsi confiées, elles prendront une valeur toute nouvelle ; néanmoins je me conformerai scrupuleusement à toute injonction en sens contraire.

Je sais fort bien qu'aucun acteur ou actrice ne peut répondre d'après une expérience personnelle à toutes les questions suivantes ; mais je crois que tous y trouveront quelques points sur lesquels il leur sera aisé de jeter de la lumière.

Si quelque acteur oublié sur ma liste veut bien m'envoyer son nom et son adresse, je lui ferai parvenir immédiatement un de ces questionnaires à remplir.

I.

Dans les situations émouvantes, les larmes vous viennent-elles aux yeux ? Les appelez-vous et les refoulez-vous à volonté ? Dans les tirades pathétiques, votre voix se brise-t-elle malgré vous ? Ou bien simulez-vous, de propos délibéré, une voix brisée ? Supposons que dans une même situation, vous versiez un soir de vraies larmes et parliez avec une réelle contraction de la gorge, et que le jour suivant vous simuliez ces phénomènes sans les éprouver : dans laquelle de ces deux occasions pensez-vous produire le plus d'effet sur votre auditoire ?

II.

Quand l'acteur Macready, après la mort d'une fille bien aimée, joua le rôle de Virginius, il avoua que le souvenir de cette enfant lui faisait verser de brûlantes larmes dans les parties les plus pathétiques du drame. Avez-vous jamais fait une expérience analogue ? Votre jeu s'est-il jamais ressenti d'un chagrin (soit récent, soit ancien) personnellement éprouvé, dans une situation qui vous en rappelait les tristes circonstances ? L'émotion éprouvée était-elle, oui ou non, à l'avantage de votre jeu ? Et quel en était l'effet sur l'auditoire ?

III.

Quand, dans la vie réelle, vous vous êtes trouvé dans une situation émouvante (au lit de mort d'un parent, par exemple) ou, par occasion, témoin d'un accident, en notez-vous sciemment les effets et les détails afin d'en faire plus tard et de sang-froid usage à la scène ? Ou bien avez-vous jamais remarqué que vous vous soyez servi à la scène d'un souvenir de la vie réelle, enregistré inconsciemment par votre mémoire ?

IV.

Dans les scènes provoquant le rire, vous amusez-vous pour votre compte ? Ou bien votre gaieté est-elle entièrement affectée ? Avez-vous jamais ri jusqu'aux larmes sur la scène ? Et dans l'un ou l'autre de ces cas, quel a été l'effet produit sur l'auditoire ? (N.B.—Il n'est pas question ici du rire provoqué par certaines méprises ou autres incidents imprévus, mais uniquement du rire qui fait partie de la trame de la pièce.)

V.

Vous est-il arrivé de rougir involontairement en représentant la timidité, la modestie, ou la honte ? de pâlir dans une scène d'épouvante ? ou bien avez-vous remarqué ces signes extérieurs chez d'autres artistes ?

VI.

Un acteur distingué me dit que généralement il transpire abondamment pendant la représentation ; mais que la transpiration varie beaucoup, non pas tant selon le degré de mouvement qu'il se donne, que selon le degré d'émotion qu'il ressent. Les soirs de représentation où il ' ne sent pas son rôle,' il joue Othello sans mouiller un fil, quoique l'effort physique soit alors au moins aussi grand que les soirs où il est baigné de sueur. Votre propre expérience est-elle d'accord avec la sienne ? La fatigue que vous occasionnent certains rôles est-elle en proportion directe avec les efforts physiques qu'ils exigent, ou bien dépend-elle des émotions que vous éprouvez ?

VII.

G. H. Lewes raconte que Macready, dans le rôle de Shylock, avait l'habitude de secouer une échelle avec violence avant d'entrer en scène avec Tubal, de façon à s'échauffer au degré voulu. Il raconte aussi qu'on surprit une fois l'acteur Liston jurant, tempêtant tout seul dans une des coulisses avant une scène de fureur comique. Avez-vous jamais trouvé qu'il fût difficile d'arriver d'un bond à l'effet voulu ? En ce cas, comment surmontez-vous cette difficulté ?

VIII.

On raconte malicieusement d'un acteur bien connu qu'il s'identifiait dès le matin avec le personnage qu'il devait jouer le soir ; quand il devait jouer Richard III, il était féroce, cynique et cruel ; tandis que, lorsqu'il devait jouer Mercutio ou Benedick, il était tout grâce, tout entrain et amabilité. Avez-vous senti chez vous pareille tendance ? L'avez-vous observée chez d'autres ? Au foyer, pendant les entr'actes, êtes-vous porté à garder le ton et l'allure du personnage que vous représentez ? Avez-vous remarqué cette dispostion chez d'autres acteurs ?

IX.

Pourriez-vous donner quelques exemples d'un état d'esprit où deux courants d'idées, et même davantage, se superposant dans votre âme, y coexistent avec la préoccupation de votre rôle ? En précisant davantage, pouvez-vous décrire comment il vous est arrivé de donner une part de vos facultés mentales aux émotions de votre rôle, tandis que d'autre part vous critiquiez minutieusement vos gestes et vos intonations, tout en vous rendant compte de l'effet que votre jeu produisait sur l'auditoire ?

X.

Diderot raconte que Lekain, dans une scène d'émotion violente, vit sur les planches la boucle d'oreille en diamant d'une actrice, et qu'il eut la présence d'esprit de l'envoyer d'un coup de pied vers l'un des portants de la scène plutôt que de l'écraser sous son pied. Pourriez-vous donner un exemple similaire de présence d'esprit ? Et regarderiez-vous ceci comme prouvant que l'acteur est resté froid malgré l'émotion qu'il simule ?

XI.

Quant aux rôles que vous avez longtemps joués : Avez-vous remarqué que cette répétition constante vous conduisait à l'insensibilité ? Faites-vous, pendant un certain nombre de représentations, des progrès, jusqu'à ce que, parvenu à un certain point, vous sentiez vos progrès s'arrêter ou même une décadence se produire ? Ou perfectionnez-vous de jour en jour votre rôle pendant une longue série de représentations ?

XII.

Cédez-vous parfois à de soudaines inspirations de geste ou d'accent qui vous arrivent lorsque vous êtes en scène ? Etes-vous capable de noter et de reproduire ensuite ces inspirations ? Avez-vous jamais produit, par pur hasard ou par méprise, d'heureux effets que vous avez ensuite incorporés à votre jeu d'une façon permanente ?

KEY TO REFERENCES.

Assézat = 'Œuvres Complètes de D. Diderot. . . . Notices, Notes &c. . . .' Par J. Assézat. Paris, 1875-77.

Aston = 'A Brief Supplement to Colley Cibber, Esq; his Lives of the late famous Actors and Actresses.' By Anthony, Vulgò Tony, Aston. London, 1747 or 1748.

Bancroft = 'Mr. and Mrs. Bancroft On and Off the Stage.' Written by Themselves. London, 1888.

Boaden = 'Memoirs of Mrs. Siddons.' By James Boaden, Esq. Second edition. London, 1831.

Boswell = 'Boswell's Life of Johnson.' Edited by George Birkbeck Hill, D.C.L. Oxford, 1887.

Bunn = 'The Stage, both Before and Behind the Curtain.' By Alfred Bunn. London, 1840.

Campardon = 'Les Comédiens du Roi de la Troupe Italienne.' Par E. Campardon. Paris, 1880.

Campbell = 'Life of Mrs. Siddons.' By Thomas Campbell. London, 1834.

Charlotte Cushman = 'Charlotte Cushman.' By Clara Erskine Clement. (American Actor Series.) London (*no date*).

Cole = 'The Life and Theatrical Times of Charles Kean, F.S.A.' By John William Cole. London, 1859.

Compton = 'Memoir of Henry Compton.' Edited by Charles and Edward Compton. London, 1879.

Coquelin = 'L'Art et le Comédien.' Par C. Coquelin. Paris, 1880.

Q

Crabb Robinson = 'Diary, Reminiscences, and Correspondence of H. Crabb Robinson.' Edited by T. Sadler. London, 1869.

Davies = ' Dramatic Miscellanies, consisting of Critical Observations on several Plays of Shakespeare.' By T. Davies. London, 1784.

D'Heylli = 'Rachel, d'après sa Correspondance.' Par Georges d'Heylli Paris, 1882.

Dibdin = 'Annals of the Edinburgh Stage.' By James C. Dibdin. Edinburgh, 1888.

Doran = 'Annals of the English Stage from Thomas Betterton to Edmund Kean.' By Dr. Doran, F.S.A. Edited by Robert W. Lowe. London, 1887.

Dorat = 'La Déclamation Théâtrale ; Poëme didactique.' [Par C. J. Dorat.] Paris, 1766.

Everard = ' Memoirs of an unfortunate Son of Thespis ; being a Sketch of the Life of Edward Cape Everard, Comedian.' Edinburgh, 1818.

Gueullette = 'Acteurs et Actrices du Temps Passé. . . . Notices.' Par C. Gueullette. Paris, 1881.

Hawkins = 'The Life of Edmund Kean.' By F. W. Hawkins. London, 1869.

Houssaye = ' La Comédienne.' Par Arsène Houssaye. Paris, 1884.

Ireland = ' Letters and Poems by the late Mr. John Henderson, with Anecdotes of his Life.' By John Ireland. London, 1786.

Lardin = Lardin's Preface to Diderot's ' Paradoxe ' in the ' Bibliothèque Nationale.'

Lemazurier = ' Galerie Historique des Acteurs du Théâtre-Français, depuis 1600 jusqu'à nos jours.' Par P. D. Lemazurier. Paris, 1810.

Lowe = ' A Bibliographical Account of English Theatrical Literature. By Robert W. Lowe. London, 1888.

Ludlow = ' Dramatic Life as I found it.' By N. M. Ludlow. St. Louis, 1880.

Macready = ' Macready's Reminiscences, and Selections from his Diaries and Letters.' Edited by Sir Frederick Pollock, Bart. London, 1875.

Malone = Malone's Historical Account of the English Stage, in Prolegomena to Variorum Shakespeare. London, 1821.

Matthews and Hutton = ' Actors and Actresses of Great Britain and the United States, from the Days of David Garrick to the Present Time.' Edited by Brander Matthews and Lawrence Hutton. New York (*no date*).

Morley = ' Diderot and the Encyclopædists.'   By John Morley.   London, 1878.

Noctes Atticæ = Beloe's Translation.   London, 1795.

Oxberry = ' Oxberry's Dramatic Biography and Histrionic Anecdotes.'   London, 1825 to 1827.

Pollock = ' The Paradox of Acting, translated with Annotations from Diderot's "Paradoxe sur le Comédien."'   By Walter Herries Pollock.   With a Preface by Henry Irving.   London, 1883.

Reynolds = ' The Life and Times of Frederick Reynolds.'   Written by Himself.   London, 1826.

Scott = Miscellaneous Prose Works of Sir Walter Scott.   Edinburgh, 1846. (See also ' Quarterly Review,' xxxiv. p. 216, June 1826.)

Talma = ' Réflexions sur Lekain et l'Art Théâtral.'   Paris, 1856.

The Voice = ' The Voice ' (Newspaper).   New York, March 1888.

INDEX.

www.ingramcontent.com/pod-product-compliance
Lightning Source LLC
Chambersburg PA
CBHW020118030726

47498CB00006B/2158